TIME TRAVELER CONFIDENTIAL:

THE APOCALYPSE

DR. BRUCE GOLDBERG

ISBN I-57968-022-4

Published by
Bruce Goldberg, Inc.
4300 Natoma Ave.
Woodland Hills, CA 91364
Telephone: (800) KARMA-4-U or FAX: (818) 704-9189
Email: drbg@sbcglobal.net
Web Site: www.drbrucegoldberg.com

Printed in the United States of America

OTHER BOOKS BY DR. BRUCE GOLDBERG

Past Lives, Future Lives

Soul Healing

The Search for Grace: A Documented Case of Murder and Reincarnation

Spirit Guide Contact Through Hypnosis

Peaceful Transition: The Art of Conscious Dying and the Liberation of the Soul

New Age Hypnosis

Past Lives, Future Lives Revealed

Unleash Your Psychic Powers

Look Younger and Live Longer: Add 25 to 50 Quality Years to Your Life, Naturally

Protected by the Light: The Complete Book of Psychic Self-Defense

Time Travelers from Our Future: A Fifth Dimension Odyssey

Astral Voyages: Mastering the Art of Interdimensional Travel

Self-Hypnosis: Easy Ways to Hypnotize Your Problems Away

Custom Design Your Own Destiny

Karmic Capitalism: A Spiritual Approach to Financial Independence

Dream Your Problems Away: Heal Yourself While You Sleep

Lose Weight Permanently and Naturally

Egypt: An Extraterrestrial and Time Traveler Experiment

ABOUT THE AUTHOR

Dr. Bruce Goldberg holds a B.A. degree in Biology and Chemistry, is a Doctor of Dental Surgery, and has an M.S. degree in Counseling Psychology. He retired from dentistry in 1989, and has concentrated on his hypnotherapy practice in Los Angeles. Dr. Goldberg was trained by the American Society of Clinical Hypnosis in the techniques and clinical applications of hypnosis in 1975.

Dr. Goldberg has interviewed on Coast to Coast AM, Oprah, Leeza, Joan Rivers, Regis, Tom Snyder, Jerry Springer, Jenny Jones, and Montel Williams shows; by CNN, NBC, Fox, CBS News, and many others.

Through lectures, television and radio appearances, and newspaper articles, including interviews in Time *The Los Angeles Times*, *USA Today*, and the *Washington Post*, he has conducted more than 35,000 past-life regressions and future-life progressions since 1974, helping thousands of patients empower themselves through these techniques. His CDs, cassette tapes and DVDs teach people self-hypnosis, and guide them into past and future lives. He gives lectures and seminars on hypnosis, regression and progression therapy, and conscious dying; he is also a consultant to corporations, attorneys, and the local and network media. His first edition of *The Search for Grace*, was made into a television movie by CBS. His third book, the award winning *Soul Healing*, is a classic on alternative medicine and psychic empowerment. *Past Lives-Future Lives* is Dr. Goldberg's international bestseller and is the first book written on future lives (progression hypnotherapy).

Dr. Goldberg distributes CDs, cassette tapes, and DVDs to teach people self-hypnosis and to guide them into past and future lives and time travel. For information on self-hypnosis tapes, speaking engagements. or private sessions. Dr. Goldberg can be contacted directly by writing to:

Bruce Goldberg, D.D.S., M.S.
4300 Natoma Avenue, Woodland Hills, CA 91364
Telephone: (800) Karma-4-U or (800) 527-6248
Fax: (818) 704-9189
Email: drbg@sbcglobal.net
Website: www.drbrucegoldberg.com

Please include a self-addressed, stamped envelope with your letter.

One

Mustafa Striker settled down behind his desk and pushed a few buttons on his hologram resonator to bring up a hologram. The Reptilian extraterrestrial on the other end didn't look very happy. In fact, Drax, as head of this planet on a far distant galaxy, never looked pleased.

"We are not yet convinced that you have the capability to succeed in your plan to create the black hole that will destroy your universe, Striker." Drax's melodramatic tone always made Striker nervous.

"I am ready to effect our plan, Drax. You needn't worry. I am well aware of how you treat those who fail." Striker recalled how his partner, Zucor, was caught stealing technical equipment to enact a different plan by government agents and was quickly disposed of by Drax's thought-wave scrambler long before a trial could be scheduled.

"In just a few days I will have all the equipment assembled and will transport it and myself back to 1999 to begin the destruction of the galaxy," Striker said. He tried to be his usual arrogant and overconfident self, but felt uneasy as he recalled the slow and painful death that Zucor had experienced. This would be his fate if he failed.

The year was 3567, and time travel had existed for over five hundred years. Drax had for several hundred years wanted Earth's galaxy destroyed. He lacked the manpower and weaponry to effect this goal through military action, so a special plan was devised.

Drax was well recognized on his planet of Reptilian beings as the Einstein of his generation. He had mastered hyperspace physics as a child, and now had devised a plan to destroy what he considered to be his chief competition, our galaxy.

The psychologically disturbed and twisted mind of Drax exhibited an unusual degree of paranoia. He made Hitler and Saddam Hussein look like pussycats in a comparison. In Drax's twisted world, Earth's galaxy had achieved a technological advancement to nearly equal that of Drax's planet. Even though Earth had no intention of threatening them, Drax felt that it was a matter of time before Earth would invade them.

Striker had never liked living on Earth. He was well trained as a scientist, but never got the recognition he felt he deserved. His application to become a time traveler, or *chrononaut*, was rejected several times by the government, and this just made him angrier. Now, at age 40, it was too late to become a time traveler, at least not legally.

A most unusual meeting had taken place two years

earlier between Striker, in his role as an ambassador, and Drax. Earth's government wanted to establish relations with Drax's planet and explore his galaxy. Drax, as the leader of his confederation, appeared receptive to this negotiation.

In reality, Drax was looking for vulnerabilities in Earth's system and a way to destroy us and Earth's galaxy. Through the use of advanced space travel technology, Striker had been sent to Drax's planet to establish political ties. Instead, Striker had made a deal with Drax to assist in the destruction of Earth's galaxy. In return for his assistance, Striker would be made head of one of their smaller planets, inhabited by humans with a similar genetic makeup. Drax and all of his planet's inhabitants were one hundred percent reptilians and never allowed interbreeding of any type. They were the ultimate racists.

Upon his return to Earth, Striker had begun to execute Drax's plan. This had to do with time travel and the creation of an uncontrollable black hole that would engulf Earth's entire galaxy. The theoretical models for this plan had originated during the latter half of the 20th-century.

Miguel Alcubierre's classic paper discussed the concept of hyper-fast space travel. He developed the principle of Alcubierre Warp Drive (AWD) as a consequence of Einstein's General Theory of Relativity. In it, Alcubierre states that space-time can be twisted, deformed, and possibly even engineered by concentrations (random or selective) of mass/energy.

Space-time is changed by AWD in such a manner

that the region directly in front of the ship contracts, while the region directly behind it expands. The net effect of this is that the ship is propelled on a weightless path through space-time.

Alcubierre's mechanism requires "exotic matter" (has negative mass and moves forward in time), not available today. This AWD would go a long way toward making interstellar travel to other planets possible, as well as time travel, by eliminating the time dilation problem. For example, a person could leave on a Monday morning and travel on a thousand-light-year journey and return the following Monday to find that everyone else (including him) had aged no more than one week.

Alcubierre's work was one of the first theoretical realizations of "metric engineering," an idea first advanced by Russian Nobel laureate Andre Sakharov and American Nobel laureate T.D. Lee, and further developed by physicist Hal Puthoff and others. NASA's breakthrough Propulsion Physics Project had been working on the theory for years.

The classic model of time travel was presented by the Cal Tech astrophysicist Kip Thorne in 1988. Thorne's research dealing with enlarging a traversable wormhole began at the request of the late Carl Sagan, who asked Thorne to research a technically accurate time machine for Sagan's novel *Contact* (which became a feature film starring Jodie Foster).

During the 1940s the German mathematician Kurt Gödel demonstrated that if we could warp space-time enough, we could create "closed time-like curves," which would function as time machines.

A black hole is an incredibly dense collapsed star—a "singularity"—with a gravitational field so strong that even light cannot escape it. Many scientists believe that massive black holes exist at the center of Earth's galaxy. Black holes are predicted by Einstein's equations.

These equations also predict the existence of a "white hole." Though white holes have not been observed in nature, it is theorized that matter being sucked into a rapidly spinning black hole could avoid the singularity, travel through a wormhole, and emerge from a white hole at the other end.

Theoretically, a wormhole is a time machine that leads to the past or future. The connection between black holes and white holes is constantly materializing and dematerializing. By entering a black hole and exiting through a white hole, matter ends up in the future. The reverse also applies.

There are several problems with attempting to use a wormhole to travel through time.

1.   Wormholes, as they are theorized to exist in nature, are microscopic.
2.   Even if this type of wormhole could be enlarged, a spaceship or human entering it could be crushed by the gravitational "throat" caused by the singularity.
3.   As a spaceship crosses the event horizon—the point at which the black hole's gravity becomes so great that

light is trapped—the difference is the
gravitational pull on different parts of
the ship would stretch it, tearing it to
pieces.
4.   The radiation sucked into the black hole
would burn any living creature to vapor.

The solution to this problem is to enlarge a
wormhole that is not associated with black holes or white
holes. Einstein showed that this would eliminate the
pinching effort by applying a special exotic matter to the
sides of this wormhole, and it could be made traversable.

Kip Thorne, Michael Morris, and Ulvi Yurtsever
worked on this model and wrote a scientific paper in
1988, published in *Physical Review Letters*. They
suggested that the exotic matter should be confined to the
central area of the wormhole around the throat, and be
surrounded by ordinary matter.

In this article they stated, "One can imagine an
advanced civilization pulling a wormhole out of the
quantum foam and enlarging it to classical size. From a
single wormhole, an infinitely advanced civilization can
make a time machine. If the laws of physics permit
traversable wormholes, then they probably also permit
such a wormhole to be transformed into a 'time
machine.'"

Other advantages to using exotic matter are a
minimizing of the stretching forces and a tremendous
decrease in the radiation levels within the wormhole.
Thus, exotic matter solves all of the current problems
with time travel. The only issue is that we had no such

exotic matter until the 31st century!

A critical problem created by the use of traversable wormholes for time travel is that it results in tears in the fabric of space-time. This explains many weather problems and Fortean phenomena, such as fish falling from the sky. Without the use of exotic matter, these tears in the fabric of space-time may become so large that they create uncontrollable effects, such as the creating of enormous black holes. Singularities are those areas of space-time where large distortions and tears in the fabric of space-time appear. These singularities exist in the centers of the black holes. The laws of physics go haywire in these singularities.

In 3050 a brilliant scientist, Taatos, enlarged a wormhole, lined it with exotic matter (as Kip Thorne's model demonstrates) and became the first time traveler, or *chrononaut*. Every time he and his team traveled back in time using this mechanism, minor tears in the fabric of space-time were created. These tears would have been enormous if no exotic matter had been utilized.

Beginning in the 35th-century, teleportation (which did not result in tears in the fabric of space-time) replaced enlarging wormholes as the mechanism of time travel. The old technology remained in storage in Taatos' original laboratory on Muvia (the risen ancient continent of Lemuria, or Mu) in the Pacific Ocean.

So Drax's plan was relatively simple. All Striker had to do was steal the 31st-century-time-travel technology from Muvia and transport himself and the equipment via a flying saucer craft back to the late 20th-century and begin enlarging wormholes without utilizing exotic matter. This would result, according to Drax's calculations, in an enormous black hole. This would take fifteen hundred years to be created and would eventually suck all planets and stars (Earth's sun is a star) into it, effectively destroying Earth's universe and eventually Earth's galaxy.

Shortly after this holographic conference, Striker piloted a small triangular craft to Muvia in his role of ambassador, requesting a tour of the old laboratory of Taatos, which was only minimally guarded, since the technology represented there was obsolete by four hundred years.

After his arrival on the old base, Striker was given a short tour by the only employee on duty. Later, when he was alone, he began to assemble the equipment and computer disks of operating data necessary for his plan.

The lone guard was confused when he returned to the lab to turn off the light. "What are you doing, Dr. Striker?" he asked.

"Oh, I am just gathering this material for an archaeological exhibit at the capital next week." Striker's face showed signs of nervousness and stress. As the guard approached Striker events took deadly turn.

"I'm going to have to clear this with my superior," the guard said as he reached for his communicator. Just then Striker kicked the guard in the groin, and as he buckled over, Striker pulled out a knife and stabbed him in the neck.

Next, he plunged the blade into the guard's gut. All Striker focused on now was the guard's eyes, open wide in horror. As he jerked the blade out, the guard buckled over onto the floor, blood spewing out of both his stomach and neck.

It took Striker nearly two hours to activate the mechanism necessary to enlarge a wormhole with sufficient size to carry him and his craft, loaded with special equipment, back in time to 1999.

The following day the guard's murder was reported to the government, and an agent was sent to Muvia with orders to find out what the crime was all about and to arrest Mustafa Striker. The agent assigned was Bob Gullon, Time Traveler Security Agent (TTSA).

Two

Bob Gullon sat at his computer and listened to his favorite music. He was constantly ridiculed by his colleagues at the Time Traveler Security Agency (TTSA) because of his obsession with music from the 1960s. Agent Gullon was more than a futuristic cop. He was a scholar of the 20th- and 21st-century and a time traveler (*chrononaut*) with nearly eighty years of experience.

Although Bob was over one hundred years old, he looked like a man in his early thirties. He was ruggedly good-looking, with blond hair, blue eyes, just a little over six feet tall, with an athletic physique and a boyish grin. Bob was clean-shaven. And he was a loner by nature.

Due to a device known as the *Alpha Syncolarium*, Bob was able to significantly slow down the aging process, and could expect to live between 500 and 900 years. All citizens of the 36th-century had access to this technology.

The Alpha Syncolarium was an isolation-tank-like structure that sent light waves through the body and adjusted sound frequencies which facilitated the body's production of the sex hormone DHEA-S (dehydroepiandrosterone sulfate). DHEA then stimulated the production of T-lymphocytes and maximized the immune system's responses. The result was an extended life span, characterized by much vitality and energy.

As he listened to the Turtles and the Four Seasons sing their songs, he reminisced on his days at the time traveler academy in Muvia. He had been twenty-five when his application for chrononaut training was accepted. As with all candidates, Bob had earned his doctorate in hyperspace physics with a dual major in quantum medicine.

After being selected through a highly competitive process (one had to be younger than thirty), he began his four-year training in Muvia. Advanced courses in quantum medicine (energy healing), hyperspace physics and history and archaeology were just some of the courses he took.

The physical-conditioning component of the curriculum was rigorous, but less demanding than in the early days of time travel (31st- through 34th-centuries), when being subjected to enlarged wormholes and singularities was the mode of time travel. Since the 35th-century, teleportation had been utilized, and the body was subjected to far less stress.

Bob mostly enjoyed the spiritual growth aspects of

his chrononaut training. This consisted of self-hypnosis, chakra balancing, psychic self-defense, and other techniques to enhance one's aura and function on a higher level. The main purpose of chrononauts was to assist others in different time periods to grow spiritually. Since 36th-century people lived in prior lives during those time periods (TTSA and the entire society of the 36th-century believed in reincarnation), by assisting others in the past they were helping themselves. 21st-century citizen could correctly say, "They are us in the future."

The Muvia base was composed of several mushroom-like structures several hundred feet high. In addition, highly advanced computerized navigation and information structures called Psiocoms could be observed. Security on the base was maintained by security personnel called Trackers, who patrolled the base in antigravity Hover Bikes. Activity was also monitored by spherical devices called Orbs, which were mini-satellites surveying the entire base.

Many miles away from the base, the original lab of Taatos had remained undisturbed for the last five hundred years. It was preserved as a museum for the chrononauts, and the public as well. It was at this site that Mustafa Striker had changed from ambassador to wanted murderer and thief.

Bob's thoughts drifted back to sixties music as he played a series of Rolling Stones and Beatles hits. He satisfied his late-afternoon hunger by concentrating on a typical 1960s meal—hamburgers and fries. His thoughts were registered in his food simulator, and his meal was ready in just two minutes. Although this was synthetic food, it was surprisingly nutritious and nonfattening. One could eat all one wanted and not gain a pound. Bob referred to this device as the "mind-wich" machine.

During his chrononaut training, Bob had studied the background of the originator of time travel, Taatos, a truly brilliant scientist, archaeologist, and writer, along with many other talents. He had done the original research on enlarging wormholes and lining them with exotic matter to allow saucer-shaped craft to travel back in time.

Initially, he had sent holographic images to other time eras. Then he had transported small objects, and finally lab animals, into the past. With these successes he volunteered to send himself back in time, and this was approved by the government after much debate. That date was 3050, and Taatos became the very first chrononaut.

He headed a team consisting of Geb, Isis, Osiris, and Horus. They spent much time in ancient Egypt and were worshipped as gods. The ancient Greeks called Taatos Hermes.

Bob recalled his early experiences with teleportation. Utilizing teleportation as a means of local travel had been around since the 25th-century. Its use in time travel had required another thousand years. When chrononaut students had their early trials with teleportation to different time periods, they were debriefed.

His first assignment had been the 28th-century, and he remembered describing his experience to his supervisor. "What was it like, Bob? Tell me in your own words." The supervisor patiently awaited Bob's response.

Bob leaned against the wall of the debriefing room, folded his arms across his chest and began. "It felt almost like I was caught in a giant web. Suddenly the world exploded into countless billions of glowing threads. They stretched away in all directions, and they intersected everything, including me. I could see the room around me, superimposed within the patterns of these threads. It seemed like I was aware of everything, although not in any detail. The overall effect was very similar to looking at a hologram, except it was visceral as well as visual. You could see and feel the image, but you could also see and feel the interference pattern. There was a very odd sense of my consciousness being split. What I mean by that is that two contradictory thoughts were present in my mind simultaneously."

"How long did these effects last?" asked his supervisor.

"They disappeared almost immediately upon my arrival at both locations."

Many times in his nearly eighty-year career as a chrononaut Bob had requested duty in the 20th- and 21st-centuries. He had been there only a dozen or so times. These assignments were mostly routine. He had always wished for an exciting assignment with global significance. Little did he know that his dream was about to be fulfilled, far beyond his expectations.

Bob didn't mind being alone. In fact, he preferred it. He had never married. Occasionally his mind raced back to three years ago when he had been engaged to Tiana Closeau.

Bob reflected back on the very first time he met Tiana. It was during a lecture given by both his parents at the World Federation of History and Archeology (WFHA). Bob's mother, being an archeologist, and his father, a historian, both worked for this organization for over one hundred years. They also taught at a local university. Their specialty was life in 20th- and 21st-century America, and this was Bob's favorite topic.

This was a long evening and during a break Bob went to get a cup of coffee at the refreshment station. He was tired and the evening was long. Bob emptied the coffee from the small long-handled pot into his cup. He thought the thick Turkish coffee would keep him alert in spite of his lack of sleep the night before.

Bob reflected on his loneliness. It had been quite awhile since he had dated and he longed for female companionship. This frustration did not affect his duties as a TTSA, but it still left him with a sense of being unfulfilled as a man.

Suddenly, a beautiful young woman approached him. She was tall and better dressed than the rest of the attendees in this 36th-century lecture. The black sweater and skirt, black stockings and flat-soled black shoes contrasted with her mane of chestnut hair, held in place by a clasp at the nape of the neck. Her skin was the color of honey. She wore no rings on her fingers and no makeup on her naturally attractive face.

"Excuse me, aren't you Bob Gullon, the son of tonight's speakers?"

"Yes," Bob responded nervously. "Who may I ask are you?"

"My name is Tiana Closeau and I am a great fan of your parents' research and your work as a chrononaut."

Her brown eyes were flecked with gold and appeared to grow lighter when she shook his hand.

The smell of her hair was fresh, salt-air fresh, and there was the smell of flowers from some distant place, soft and pleasant, that made Bob think of being off the Florida Keys, on a warm spring night, going someplace, yet no place special, just enjoying the long, soft moments.

As Bob shook Tiana's band he could feel the warmth of her body and under his fingers a tiny pulse was racing much faster than he would've expected.

"I can understand your knowledge of my parent's work, but how is it you know of my work?"

"I work for the Federation Embassy, and we are familiar with the backgrounds of all the chrononauts. You are known as one of the more resourceful and outspoken time travelers," she pursed her lips and looked up at Bob, as he was four inches taller than Tiana.

Bob felt a bit like a defendant on the witness stand, yet his responses to Tiana. were as polite and accurate as possible. Just then an odd-looking nerdy man appeared and approached Tiana. He was a gangly, tall guy with hips like doorknobs and unruly, brittle hair that looked like he styled it by sticking his head in a toilet bowl and flushing. His cracked, high-pitched mess of a voice sounded like the perpetual angry whine of a teenage girl. He wore Coke-bottle glasses that made his eyes bulge like a frog's, and he had the fashion sense of an accordionist in a polka band.

"Hi," said the nerd, facing Tiana and purposely ignoring Bob. "I couldn't help noticing you in this crowded auditorium. I would like to get to know you better."

Tiana faced the nerd and calmly turned around to face Bob. "I'm sorry, but I found the only person in this building that I would like to know better," she declared.

With that remark the nerd left. Now there was just Tiana and Bob, staring hungrily at each other. At this moment Bob was oblivious to the rest of the world. There is a single, tiny comer of the mind that insists on calling up trivial bits of useless knowledge at the most inappropriate moments, suspended in unreality. Bob found himself taking refuge in that comer as he recalled this first meeting with Tiana.

Bob's parents had told him many years ago that when Magellan's ships had first appeared at Patagonia, the local Indians couldn't see them. This was because their minds bad been unable to process what their eyes were reporting. Their Stone Age reality structure had simply not included anything like those ships.

When Tiana continued their short conversation Bob's mind was unaware of everyone and everything else in the auditorium. It was most fortunate that Tiana left him with her contact information, as Bob just wasn't thinking straight. Tiana had a hypnotic effect upon him.

They started dating immediately. Bob had never known anyone quite like Tiana. She was bright, beautiful and sensuous in all respects. She confided in Bob about

her dysfunctional family background. Her alcoholic
father abused her psychologically and sexually during her
formative years. Bob was always a sucker for a damsel in
distress. He greatly respected Tiana's growth in
overcoming that handicap and focusing on her career
with the embassy.

Tiana shared many of Bob's interest. She also
favored the 20th-century, loved sixties music, and
hamburgers and fries. Bob was in heaven. He recalled
taking her to her home after their first real date.

They rode an escalator up from an underground
GRAV-Tube station and emerged onto a sidewalk (a
moving sidewalk). Suddenly, Bob was staring at a two-
hundred-story tower rising before them. They then
walked into a lobby large enough to park a small
spaceship. Next, they entered one of fifty vertical tubes
and stepped off into a quiet corridor lined with closed
doors.

As soon as they entered Tiana's apartment and
closed the door behind them, Tiana pinned Bob against
the wall and buried her tongue into his mouth. Her left
hand grasped the back of his head tightly, with her right
hand exploring his body like a small, hungry animal.

Tiana stepped back and stared at Bob for a few, yet
eternal, moments. She then removed her blouse and held
it in her left hand as she marched toward the bedroom.
Suddenly, she turned around to face Bob.

"You're not moving," she said.

"I'm enjoying the view," replied Bob.

"When you're done admiring the view, join me m
the bedroom," Tiana teased.

"Right behind you, honey," Bob said and followed her into the bedroom.

Tiana sat on her bed and removed the rest of her clothes. She ran both hands through her hair, arching her back, her rib cage pressing against her skin. She then ran her hands over her abdomen and motioned Bob to come to her.

When Bob disrobed and climbed onto the bed they made love for the first time. It was one of the most exquisite and disconcerting experiences of his life. Their palms flattened against each other and their forearms followed suit at every point along his body, his flesh and bone pressed against hers.

Next, her thighs rose up to his hips and she took him inside of her as her legs slid down the backs of his and her heels clamped just below his knees. Bob felt utterly enveloped, as if he melted through her flesh. She cried out in ecstasy and Bob could feel as if it had come from his own vocal chords.

The sounds of their lovemaking still echoed in Bob's ears. She had a scar on her right thigh, as a result of her alcoholic father's burning her with a pen flashlight laser while forcing himself upon her.

Bob ran his tongue over the scar.

"Mmm," she said, "do that again."

"Can a scar be erogenous?" Bob asked.

"I think anything can be erogenous," she coyly replied.

"Does this bring back bad memories of your youth?" Bob asked.

"I do my best to block out those days. It's not easy to forget being raped repeatedly, especially by my father."

Bob raised his right hand and used the backs of his fingers to brush a strand of Tiana's hair off her forehead. He then allowed the fingers to drop slowly down the edge of her face, along the soft warmth of her throat, and then the small, firm curve of her right breast. He grazed her nipple with his palm and moved his hand back up her face and pulled her down on top of him. He held her so tightly for a moment that he could hear their hearts drumming through their chests.

"Your father, he's dead, right?" Bob asked.

She nodded yes.

Then they fell asleep. When Bob awoke the following morning Tiana' s body shifted and her legs were curled over his, wrapped tightly between his thighs. Her head was tucked into his shoulder, her left hand draped across his chest. Her breath fluttered against Bob's neck, rhythmic with sleep.

The way she folded herself into his arms was so natural he could hardly believe it. Women were something he had never needed. They were always there. but he bad never felt the desire to keep one around very long. On occasions they were very useful, but generally speaking. there was very little they could do that he couldn't do better and faster, without having to be perpetually obligated.

One Sunday just a little over three years ago she was killed inside her apartment when Bob was out of town on assignment. Her body was found two days later by her maid. The case still remains unsolved, and it had taken Bob nearly two years to get over Tiana's death. During the last year he had begun to date sporadically, but never became involved seriously with anyone. Being married to his work suited him just fine.

The instant message on his computer came on unexpected: YOU ARE TO REPORT IMMEDIATELY TO AGENT SISTERN. Nova Sistern was Bob's supervisor, and had the split personality of a hard-nosed government official superimposed on an emotional and sentimental woman's persona. Although she had the appearance of an attractive and physically fit 40-year-old woman, she was actually one-hundred-fifty-years old.

Nova had been Bob's supervisor for over twenty-five years, and knew him better than anyone else. There was nothing romantic between them, but she looked out for Bob and was always supportive.

Bob quickly turned off his computer and entered his teleportation station in the rear of his apartment. He instantly arrived in Nova's office and patiently waited for her robot secretary to signal him in to her private office.

Nova's office was in reality quite small in this government complex. Through the application of virtual reality techniques, it was made to appear at least four times its actual size. This always amazed Bob.

"Why have you summoned me, Nova? I was just enjoying some delightful music." Bob's displeasure at being inconvenienced was duly noted.

"I'll bet you had the Stones and Insects, um, Beatles, on with a burger and fries. Right?" She glared at Bob with a look of arrogance.

"Maybe so, but at least my apartment is larger than a peanut shell," he said as he glanced around Nova's office.

"Virtual reality techniques may not fool you, hotshot, but I have an assignment that I know will perk your interests," she said coyly as she leaned forward. She went on to explain the details of Striker's action and the murder of the guard at the Muvia museum.

"So why are you calling me in on this murder case? In case you forgot, I am a chrononaut, not Columbo or Kojak," Bob said, feeling that he now had the upper hand with her for once in his life.

"Must you always use 20th-century metaphors? Your assignment is not just to arrest Striker, but to find out what he is up to with the old wormhole technology back there," she said.

"Back where?"

"Oh, didn't I mention it?" A wry grin appeared on Nova's face. "He's back in the year 1999, give or take."

"What do you mean, give or take?" he said, now very excited about this assignment.

"We know he went back to 1999, but our intel states that the critical year to send you back is 2005. Any problems with that?"

"No, not at all, Nova. First, I will want to check out the murder scene at the museum. Has forensics been there yet?"

"Way ahead of you, hotshot. Make sure you inventory everything he took with him to the 21st-century."

"Will do, chief," he said, giving a military salute.

"Don't call me chief. I will maintain communication with you by our usual hologram resonator. Don't forget to bring it, hotshot."

As Bob moved to leave Nova's office, he could see her burying herself in a pile of computer disks dealing with a multitude of matters. This was one aspect of her position that made him happy to be a field agent. Such mundane and bureaucratic details always bored and frustrated him. He had never wanted to be assigned to any office as a supervisor.

Bob returned to his apartment and gathered his usual investigative equipment. About an hour later he teleported to the Muvia museum and went through its new tightened-up security checkpoint.

"Agent Gullon, TTSA, to check out the crime scene. I'm alone and have clearance level G8-I," he said. He had been through this procedure thousands of times during his career. The electronic scanner that encircled his body always left him with a tingly sensation.

"You are cleared," grumbled the guard. "You will notice additional personnel present. I'll let them know who you are so you can do your job without interruption."

"Thanks. Please keep me posted if anyone else will be in Taatos' old lab," Bob said. He knew that his statement was redundant, but decided on maintaining a serious and professional demeanor in light of the fact that one of the guard's colleagues and possibly a friend had been murdered the night before by Striker.

As Bob entered Taatos' laboratory, he had a sense of distant recognition. As a chrononaut academy student eighty years earlier, he had been given a guided tour of this facility. He had never been back since, and this was a most unusual homecoming.

The forensic team and homicide detectives did their job well, Bob noted. He began an inventory of items that Striker had taken with him. The list was completed within an hour. These items all dealt with 400-year-old time-travel technology. One thing Bob could not inventory was current 36th-century technology that Striker would invariably bring with him to 1999.

Bob looked around in Taatos' old lab for another two hours, searching for clues. He wasn't so concerned with the murder scene itself. That was not his department. The homicide detectives were quite competent at digging up any physical evidence required for Striker's eventual prosecution. Bob was looking for something else. What could Mustafa Striker be up to? Why did he sacrifice a promising career as an ambassador to become a fugitive and face trial for murder? Just what was the attraction for the early 21st-century anyway?

As Bob surveyed the lab he felt a certain sense of history. The lab contained relics of times past, but was still impressive. The heritage of time travel and the man who discovered it filled the building.

He decided to change the chip in the teleporting device attached to his belt. Suddenly the chip rolled away from him and ended up over a hundred feet away from the guard's body, outlined in infrared light. It was lying against the wall at a 60-degree angle. As Bob retrieved the disk, he noted that it magnetically attracted another disk formerly wedged against the wall. This made him suspect that the disk might have been dropped by Striker in his hasty departure following the guard's murder. The disk also appeared to be part of a current holographic resonator and not part of the museum's exhibits. He placed it in his pocket for further study later.

Having completed his survey and inventory, Bob left the lab and teleported back to his apartment to make preparations for his trip back to 2005. He arrived in moments, and his thoughts were dominated by life in the early 21st-century. Instead of synthetic hamburger and French fries, he would soon enjoy the real thing. His favorite burger place was the In-N-Out Burger franchise, with branches all throughout Southern California. Nova had informed him that his destination was Los Angeles in 2005. His mind raced to the last time he had devoured a real hamburger and French fries. It had been almost ten years since he had visited the 21st-century.

But now his attention was redirected back to the assignment. Bob placed the disk he had removed from Taatos' lab in his holographic resonator and anxiously awaited its message. What he saw and heard shocked him. Drax's image was shown in a boardroom filled with reptilians. The message was brief: OUR PLAN IS FLAWLESS. DO NOT FAIL US, STRIKER, OR YOU WILL JOIN THE REST OF YOUR KIND—DEAD.

Bob wasn't a diplomat, but his briefings informed him of who Drax was and Drax's militant nature. Drax's government had broken off diplomatic relations with Earth. This was a possible prelude to an invasion. Bob's briefings had also informed him that Drax's forces were far too small to effect a military takeover.

Nonetheless, it was his duty to turn this disk over to Nova and let the intelligence people handle it. He knew that espionage and treason charges would be added to Striker's theft and murder allegations.

Bob quickly teleported the disk to Nova and awaited her instructions. He knew it wouldn't be long if she wasn't in a meeting. For now he continued with preparations for his trip to sunny California in 2005.

Forty-five minutes later the expected response from Nova arrived in the form of a hologram. Bob sat at his desk and opened the files. He could now communicate with her as she gave him his orders.

"I assume you played the disk," Nova said nervously.

"Yes, and I am aware of the repercussions of the missions. This is far beyond a simple murder and theft."

"No kidding. The entire safety of this planet could be at stake! We're sending you to 2005 to stop him at whatever he is attempting. By that time his plan should be under way and you can use your wits and other skills to prevent this war, or whatever," said Nova.

Bob never questioned his own achievements or accepted unjustified flattery. "I appreciate your faith and confidence, Nova. As soon as I find out what he is up to, I will let you in on his plans. Thanks for the extra equipment you teleported earlier. I'm going to need all the help I can get."

Three

Michele Peterman was not your typical FBI special agent. She impressed everyone as an emotional and sensitive individual who truly cared about people. Her more hardnosed colleagues often ridiculed her and labeled her "airy-fairy.com."

In reality, Michele was one tough cookie. She was small and slender, with a heart-shaped face, white-blonde hair combed into bangs, and catlike green eyes. Her martial-arts expertise (a black belt in karate) and marksmanship with her gun more than spoke for her ability to take care of herself.

Michele's record with the agency was excellent. She received promotions and commendations in record time and was considered one of the top agents in Los Angeles in the year 2005. One of the reasons for her "airy-fairy" label came from her beliefs, which she was more than happy to share with her colleagues.

She believed in soulmates, reincarnation, and time travel. UFOs, extraterrestrials, and psychic skills were also a part of her reading and philosophy. These topics didn't go down well at the FBI. Still, Michele was the first to exercise her First Amendment rights and relate her recent readings, seminar experiences, and other acquired New Age data to her associates.

Things had been rather slow at her office lately, and Michele was anxious to sink her teeth into a big case. At the ripe young age of twenty-eight she routinely exhibited a childlike curiosity and high energy demeanor. She had always exhibited a high level of psychic awareness. This explained her metaphysical orientation toward life. Her sixth sense informed her that this was to be a most unusual and rewarding day at the office.

As Michele sped her way in her BMW to the Federal Building on Wilshire Boulevard, she had an imaginary conversation with her boss, Assistant Director Drake Collins. In this exchange she was given a plum assignment involving national security.

After arriving at her office and gulping her second cup of Starbucks coffee, Michele responded to the telephone ringing on her desk. It was Drake Collins calling.

"Yes, sir, this is Peterman. What can I do for you?" she said anxiously.

"Come into my office immediately. I have a new assignment for you."

Michele arrived at Collins' office within five minutes, and was immediately sent in by his secretary.

Collins always made a production of a briefing or case assignment. In college he had majored in theater, and had performed in at least two dozen plays before entering law school.

"Agent Peterman," he said staring at some point beyond Michele as though she was not there." I want you to begin investigating Mannaco immediately."

Michele couldn't believe her ears. Mannaco was a well-known philanthropic private corporation founded by its current CEO, Mustafa Striker. Just eighteen months ago Mannaco had announced its latest drug, which cured cancer. Subsequent tests had verified this drug's ability to rid mankind of its number two killer, second only to heart disease.

Michele had only superficially followed Mannaco's progress since it was formed in 1999. This originally small company had developed an environmentally friendly alternative to fossil fuels and had quickly grown into a multibillion-dollar corporation.

Striker was an odd man. Michele knew that he refused to take his company public and maintained a high level of secrecy concerning its various activities. She was aware of his low public profile and his ruthless reputation, but didn't think much of it. Now, she thought, there must be some heavy criminal activity for the FBI to become involved.

"What has he done to bring our agency into this matter?" she asked, nervously.

"He and his company, according to our intel, have been linked to money laundering and murder," said Collins.

"You just can't trust anybody these days. Mannaco has given hundreds of millions to charities and is one of America's most respected philanthropic organizations," Michele responded as she sat upright in her chair and brushed her bangs away from her eyes.

"This is a very sensitive matter," he said. "Only a few of our people are aware of this intel. We don't want to arrest one of America's most respected and beloved entrepreneurs without one hell of a lot of evidence. I couldn't believe this myself yesterday when I first heard it."

"Who else is going to be assigned to this case, sir?" she asked with a note of anticipation.

"No one at this time. I want to keep this as quiet as I can until we have some evidence. If this is all bullshit, I don't want to embarrass either Striker or this agency, understand?" His condescending tone always made Michele nervous.

Michele left Collins' office with a sense of confirmation regarding her psychic intuition, superimposed upon a dread of this assignment. If she in any way messed this up, she would be in big trouble. Her first step would be thorough research on Mannaco and Mustafa Striker.

Research can be tedious and boring for even the most dedicated of souls. Michele first read everything she could from various governmental agencies and the public press regarding Striker. He said he had earned a Ph.D. in biochemistry from a now-defunct university in South America. Although his academic credentials could not be confirmed, his achievements most certainly could.

During the fall of 1999 Striker had arrived in California and set up Mannaco as a small pharmaceutical research company. According to his representatives (he himself refused all interviews), Mannaco derived its name from the Bible's story of a substance miraculously supplied as food for the Israelites during the Exodus. Manna was also equated with the Philosopher's Stone, the chemical that changed base metals into silver or gold and had been popularized by medieval alchemists.

Striker claimed to have discovered this white powder that eluded the ancients, called manna or the Philosopher's Stone. *Materia prima* and *magnum opus* were other names used to describe the Philosopher's Stone. Many formulas for the substance had been devised over the centuries, usually either containing a silver or gold alloy which could be changed again into the pure metal, making alchemists believe that the metal had been transformed, or a white or yellow metallic alloy superficially resembling silver or gold. Only a small quantity of the Philosopher's Stone was said to be required in order to transform large quantities of base metals into gold. It was known not only as a transmuting agent, but also as a source of wisdom and of healing.

The Philosopher's Stone's power as a healer and a restorer of life was exemplified in legends of the "Elixir of Life," a solution of the Stone in spirits of wine which, when consumed by the alchemist, would restore health and youth. It was not supposed to prevent death, but rather to delay it, cleansing the body of impurities, prolonging life and restoring youth. It represented the purity and sanctity of the highest realm of pure thought and altruistic existence, the final outcome of man's inner transformation, of the conversion of the base metal of his outer character to the golden properties of his higher self.

In the spring of 2000 Mannaco had released an environmentally friendly alternative to fossil fuel. This technology resulted from transforming gold and platinum into a monatomic state, creating a fine white powder. The release of this fuel created quite a stir. Several oil companies immediately raised an objection, as did two congressmen and one senator. Mysteriously, the CEOs of three of these oil-company adversaries and the two congressmen and the senator were found dead within two months of Mannaco's announcement. Although the deaths were ruled suspicious, no arrests were made, and the respective investigations were quietly ended.

Mannaco quickly became a multi-billion-dollar private corporation with a large new complex located in the San Fernando Valley near the Van Nuys airport. The Securities and Exchange Commission's bullion prospectus further buttressed Mannaco's credibility when it said, "Future applications for gold, especially in its monatomic state, are in pollution control, clean energy generation, and fuel-cell technology."

Scientific journals in Italy, Spain, Germany, France, Switzerland, Singapore, England, and America had headlines such as "The Amazing Properties of Monatomic Gold."

Following this initial success, Mannaco began using this nano-gold, as it was labeled, to treat dyslexia and attention-deficit disorders. The EEG brain scans of these patients showed a synchronization of the left and right brain hemispheres. This resulted in heightened learning ability and memory, increased creativity, and a substantial resistance to stress.

Other products that Mannaco had provided during its brief history consisted of refrigerators that kept track of food essentials and either printed out a shopping list or electrically transmitted the order to a home-delivery service. In addition, the firm came up with robotic lawn mowers, sleeping machines that produced peaceful sleep, implanted biochips to enhance vision and eliminated the need for glasses, other biochips to reverse spinal-cord injuries, and genetic therapies to cure male pattern baldness.

Mannaco's recent cancer cure had added more billions to its coffers. Striker was reportedly a megalomaniac who was ruthless and shy of publicity. Although his company had been on the covers of *Time*, *Newsweek*, and *People Magazine*, and featured on all the major TV networks, Striker was never interviewed. He always sent a different department head or other representative. This mystery man had become one of the richest men in the world in just over five years. That alone was enough to generate the interest of various government agencies.

Michele wondered why Striker wasn't questioned regarding the murders of the oil-company CEOs, congressmen and senator. He definitely had the most to gain by their demise. Her sources quietly informed her that very powerful figures in the government had rushed in and quieted the investigation. She was told flatly that Striker had many high-ranking political contacts and that the deaths appeared to be likely more professional "hits."

This stimulated Michele's interest, because she felt that Striker had criminal contacts to go along with his obvious political friends. She decided that a visit to his laboratory was in order and she would go alone. Her purpose would be to snoop around and try to come up with a lead or two that could result in evidence against Striker.

Bob Gullon awoke in his Woodland Hills home, rented by the agency. This place functioned as a safe house for chrononauts in Los Angeles. Its isolated location south of Ventura Boulevard and its average appearance made it perfect for Bob to function without drawing attention to himself.

The house was a rancher with three bedrooms, two of which had been converted into offices filled with sophisticated electronic equipment. One of the most important devices at Bob's disposal was the hologram resonator that he used to communicate with his boss, Nova.

Other very advanced computers allowed him to research Striker and Mannaco thoroughly. He spent the next four hours acquainting himself with Striker's movements and accomplishments during the previous five years.

None of this helped him with what he was most seeking—Drax's plan and Striker's involvement in that plan. Suddenly a familiar hologram and voice appeared on his holographic resonator.

"Hey, hotshot, why have you not checked in?" barked Nova.

"Look, my dear, I have spent a good part of today settling in and brushing up on our friend and murderer, thief and spy, Mustafa Striker. He has been a busy camper."

"Any progress in this idiot's plan?"

"No, not yet. I'm on my way to his lab in Van Nuys to do a little observing, invisibly, of course."

"Now I know you can use your teleportation unit to stay in the fifth dimension and remain invisible to everyone else, but remember our policy: We don't want 21st-century citizens seeing you disappear into the fabric of space-time and reappearing at will. You are not working with any agency from the 21st-century, just us," Nova reminded him.

"I am well aware of that. I doubt that Striker's employees know of his 36th-century origins. Remember, I have worked in this century and location before. Trust me to do my job," Bob countered.

"OK, hotshot. I'm behind you. Let me know as soon as you find out something worthwhile."

Bob signed off and decided to stop off at In-N-Out Burger for some old-fashioned hamburgers and fries before visiting Mannaco's laboratory.

Michele Peterman loved her cat, Sheba, a short-haired female British black cat whom Michele often described as "smart as a whip." When she entered her apartment and forgot to check her messages on her digital answering machine, Sheba would scratch the floor incessantly until Michele retrieved her messages.

Such was the case today. There was only one message, and it was from her gardener, Sanchez. He calmly informed her that he was returning to Mexico and would no longer be doing the gardening at her garden apartment. She would have to find somebody else.

Having far more important things on her mind, Michele drove to Mannaco's lab in Van Nuys. It was now late afternoon and many of the lab's employees had gone home. She was not able to obtain a search warrant as instructed by Collins, so she decided to fake an ID and just snoop around.

She was surprised at how easy it was to gain entrance to the lab. All she had to do was flash her phony ID to a half-awake, overweight, and expressionless guard, and she was greeted by a reception desk with an empty seat. She made her way through a large open area that led to a labyrinth of interconnected corridors.

At about 6 p.m. the lab began to empty out. Michele decided the best thing she could do was to check computer records of the company's activities. At the end of a long, straight and seemingly endless passage she could see a sign that said RECORDS.

After what seemed like an eternity, she reached the Records door and used a small electronic device to open it. Just as she was about to enter the room, the door opened adjacent to the Records office and the chief of security, Otto Schmidt, stepped out into the hallway and immediately spotted her.

Schmidt functioned as Mustafa Striker's personal bodyguard. He also headed the security of the lab and took personal pride in doing everything he could to protect his boss and Mannaco.

He carried a Walther PPK gun in a shoulder holster under his jacket, and every so often would run his fingers over its polished stainless-steel finish. He loved his gun. Its 6.1-inch length and 20.8-ounce weight made it ideal for concealment.

The Walther PPK was a semi-automatic gun with a seven-round magazine that had a delivery like a brick through a plate-glass window. Schmidt used a Braush silencer, which offered very little reduction in muzzle velocity when applied. He preferred this older model versus the newer, larger and bulkier Walther P99, which was 7.1 inches long and weighed 21.5 ounces.

Schmidt knew very well the history of the Walther PPK. It was originally marketed as a pistol for the German undercover criminal police during the 1930s. The PPK stood for Polizei Pistole Kriminal. Anything that had the word "criminal" in it attracted him, since he loved being one. Even though his gun had been developed to stop criminals, he had successfully used it to kill police of various types on two continents.

Schmidt immediately confronted Michele and ran up to her just as she was about to enter the Records office. Before he could reach for his gun, Michele lowered her shoulders like a football player and slammed him against the wall. Stunned, he fell to the floor.

Michele raced down the corridor and rounded the first corner, then another. She was like a lab rat caught in a maze. Suddenly she heard footsteps on the highly polished tile floor and realized that Schmidt was in pursuit of her. She came to a dead-end corridor with a closed heavy steel door.

As she tried the door she cursed as it was locked and she was trapped. Exhausted and confused, she pulled her gun from her purse. Schmidt fired a shot at her that barely missed her head.

"Drop your weapon. My name is Special Agent Michele Peterman and I work for the FBI. You will be under arrest if you don't cooperate now!" she shouted.

Schmidt ignored her demands and fired a second shot, which landed less than six inches from her shoulder. Michele tried to return his fire, but was shocked to discover that her gun had jammed.

"So you're FBI, huh? A pig is a pig what is a pig. Hey, honey, have you done any research on me?" growled Schmidt.

"No. Why do you ask?"

"Oh, I just thought you'd like to know something about the man who is about to kill you."

"And just what's that?" responded Michele, trying her best not to show fear.

"I've got the letters f-l-i-o-n tattooed on my penis."

"Flion?" what the hell does that mean?"

"It only reads that when my dick is limp. When I am about to waste someone, I get a hard-on, as I have now, and it says 'Fuck the Federal Bureau of Investigation.' Bye-bye, bitch."

It is said that everything appears to move in slow motion when you are involved in a car accident. People have described seeing their lives unfold before their inner eyes when faced with a life-and-death event without regard to time elapsing. That is what Michele experienced as Schmidt pointed his gun directly at her heart and was about to pull the trigger of his Walther PPK.

Bob Gullon observed this scene from the fifth dimension. He had teleported to the lab just fifteen minutes before and decided to remain invisible in the fifth dimension, as the frequency vibrational rate of his body was far higher than everything else in our three-dimensional world, rendering him invisible.

It was now time to return to the three-dimensional world of Michele and Schmidt. Bob didn't know who Michele was prior to her pronouncement as an agent working for the FBI, but he knew he couldn't just let her die.

Just as Schmidt placed his finger on the trigger, Bob pressed a certain section of his belt buckle and a luminous red ball was projected that surrounded Schmidt, placed the guard in a state of suspended animation, and made the semi-automatic weapon nonfunctional.

Michele watched this scenario and couldn't believe her eyes. She just stood there and stared at Bob.

"Listen, we have to get out of here fast. That guard will return to normal consciousness in about ten minutes," ordered Bob.

"Just who the hell are you, and what exactly did I just witness?" she said.

"I'll answer your questions later. Follow me."

He led Michele back to the reception desk and projected another luminous red ball at the receptionist and the security guard, placing them both in suspended animation. They left the lab and Bob realized it wouldn't be a good idea to leave Michele without somehow debriefing her.

"Look, I don't have my car here. Can you drop me off somewhere so we can have a chat?" he said.

"What did you do, hitchhike here? Not on your life, you red ball-projecting freak! Look, I'm sorry for that last remark. It's just that I don't know who or what you are, and I need time to sort this out. It's Friday evening now. Take my card and call my office on Monday morning."

Michele went to her car and drove back to her Brentwood apartment. Bob watched her leave, then turned his teleporter unit on. It instantly noted Michele's position and functioned like a homing signal. The only thing Michele would think of during the long trip home was what happened and just who the strange man was.

It took over an hour to make it home to her apartment with Friday evening traffic. No e-mails or telephone messages greeted her. Sheba was sleeping on her favorite pillow on the couch and didn't bother to move from her position when Michele arrived.

Suddenly a knock at her front door startled the cat. Michele looked through her peephole and shouted, "How the hell did you find me? I made sure I wasn't followed."

Bob stood at the door and patiently responded, "May I come in? We have much to discuss."

Michele opened the door, with Sheba standing right next to her in a protective position. As Bob entered the apartment, Sheba went up to him, rubbed against his legs and purred affectionately.

"That's odd. Sheba normally shies away from

strangers, especially men. You are an odd man, aren't you?" Michele said.

"First, my name is Bob Gullon, and I also work for a government agency, but not yours."

"How do you do, Bob. By the way, thanks for saving my life. Don't tell me you're CIA."

"No. You wouldn't be familiar with my agency."

"What do you mean? I work for a national security agency called the FBI and am familiar with all security agencies. Are you NSA?"

"No. Aren't you just a little bit taken aback about how I saved your life? Remember the luminous red ball and the suspended animation effect?"

"Yeah, I was about to get to that. What was it, hypnosis?" Michele inquired.

"No, just very advanced technology. Let me see your gun."

Michele handed over her nonfunctional weapon and observed him removing a few tools from his jacket pocket and working on the gun. Within two minutes it was working perfectly.

"Here is your gun back. Put it in a safe place. You may need it soon," he said.

"Look, before you tell me some weird stuff I'm going to brew some coffee. Would you like some?" she asked.

"Sure."

Michele went into the kitchen and poured some coffee grounds into a French Melior plunger coffee maker. She returned her gun to her purse and returned to the living room, where Bob was sitting on her couch.

A few minutes later she returned to the kitchen and poured some coffee.

"Cream and sugar?" she asked.

"Yes, please."

Bob got up to receive his coffee, and his attention was directed to a bookshelf next to her television. He picked up two of the books.

"I notice you read books like *Soulmates* by Jess Stearn and *Past Lives, Future Lives Revealed* by Dr. Bruce Goldberg. Do you believe in reincarnation and time travelers from our future?"

"As a matter of fact, I am a true New Ager. How did you know about the time travelers?" she said

"Dr. Goldberg's work is very well known to me and my agency. I'm surprised you don't have a copy of his *Time Travelers from Our Future*."

"I did, but I loaned it to a friend who hasn't yet returned it. Now tell me who you work for."

"What I am about to tell you will shock you and seem totally unbelievable. I respectfully ask you to be patient with me. Is that agreeable?"

"Okay."

"I could just as easily have placed you in suspended animation when I saved you from the guard. I didn't, because when you announced yourself as an FBI agent I felt you could be of great assistance to me in my mission," Bob said.

"Just what is your mission?" she asked quietly.

"Before I get to that, I need to tell you where I am from. I am from the 36th-century and I work for the Time Traveler Security Agency."

Michele stared at Bob's deep blue eyes and strong, chiseled features, looking for body language signs that might show him to be lying. She observed none.

"You know I believe in time travelers, but this is just too much to accept. You'll have to excuse me for a moment. I need to use the ladies' room," she said.

Michele, not sure if she had a madman on her hands, went into her bedroom. She closed the door, then dropped back against the wall. She wondered what she'd gotten herself into as she checked her revolver. Finally, she went into the bathroom and fixed her face. She returned to the living room and now somehow felt more at ease with Bob.

"Before I answer a myriad questions, please tell me why you were in the lab today," he said.

"I am also on an assignment. The FBI is very interested in Mustafa Striker. I came to the lab to snoop around."

"Then we most definitely have a common interest. Why didn't you arrest the guard for attempted murder?"

"Otto Schmidt is a little fish. The bureau does not want to commit itself to showing its suspicions regarding Striker yet. I thought it best to keep a low profile until hard evidence could be contained," she said.

"So announcing you're from the FBI and possibly getting killed at Mannaco is your idea of a low profile?"

"All right, I admit to acting a little hostile. Now don't assume I believe you are a time traveler yet, but keep talking."

"What if you knew something bad was going to happen, but you couldn't tell anybody because they wouldn't believe you?" Bob said.

"You mean, like your friends are going to commit a crime and they expect you to be part of it?"

"Not quite."

"Well, I would stop them," Michele answered.

They stared at each other for a long, uncertain moment. Bob broke the silence.

"Mustafa is from my century. He murdered someone and stole valuable scientific equipment and brought it back to your time. We don't know what he is up to, but it can't be good. My assignment is to bring him back to the 36th-century to stand trial."

"Is that it?" she asked.

"No, there is more. I must find out exactly what his plan is. Also, Striker has been here for five years and each act he engages in can seriously affect the space-time continuum and the future of this planet."

"Exactly how can he do that?"

"I don't know that yet. It is most fortunate that your agency is in no rush to arrest Striker," Bob said.

"You don't really think the FBI is going to help anyone claiming to be a time traveler, do you?"

"Of course not. I only need your assistance."

"Now what can you tell me to prove beyond any doubt that you are from the future?" she asked.

"Look, I can tell you quite a bit about the technology of the future. I know that won't convince you, because you could just as easily assume I am making it up."

"So what is your solution?" she queried skeptically.

"I am going to return to my place and research an event that only a futuristic individual could know. Are you a sports fan?"

"Yes, but what does that have to do with the price of corn?" Michele said.

"I will detail the scoring and major highlights of one of your football games and baseball playoffs to be played on Sunday. These results will be given to you the day before, on Saturday. Fair enough?"

"Sure, that would do it. I must warn you in advance that it better be detailed and accurate. Here is my home fax number."

Bob left Michele's apartment and immediately teleported back to his safe house in Woodland Hills. Outside Michele's apartment, and several hundred feet above it, a black helicopter hovered. In it, Mustafa Striker and Otto Schmidt, who was piloting the craft, stared down at her apartment.

"How much do you think she knows, sir?" Otto asked.

"I don't know yet. Since she didn't have a search warrant and didn't arrest you, I can only assume not much. I am far more concerned with what Bob Gullon and the TTSA know," said Striker.

Four

Bob awoke very early on Saturday morning. His alarm clock read 6:21 A.M. He awoke fresh and alive, as though he had just come in from a brisk walk. He became aware of the musky scent of new-mown clover in the cool morning air. The sounds of birds calling to one another filled him with a sense of peace. Suddenly, Bob was startled by a covey of birds as they took to the air.

Bob's mind again drifted to his late fiancée, Tiana Closeau. He recalled the last time he saw her. When he approached her door he could hear her angelic voice in a soft, confident whisper, a whisper that knew a listener would have to lean in to hear, if necessary. "Please, come in," she said.

When Bob entered her apartment he immediately smelled the gourmet meal she had prepared. He noted the blond Scandinavian wood of the kitchen furniture and the muted reds and browns of the Persian rugs placed strategically over the hardwood floor. The sense of color gave the place an air of warmth.

After dinner they talked and went to the living room where Bob put on some of the sixties music they both loved. She gave him a hungry smile, as her spine arched and she pulled rum to her. When he kissed her it was a warm touch that began to blaze and when he pulled his mouth away he could say nothing at all for a full minute. He could still taste her and her eyes were watching him. waiting for him to speak.

"I can't believe we will be officially married in two months," Bob stated.

"Are you getting cold feet?" asked Tiana.

"No, not on your life, my embassy sweetie," responded Bob.

"It will be nice to see your parents again. Too bad my mother died in that earthquake five years ago. She would've loved you too," Tiana became emotional at the thought of her mother.

They went into her bedroom and made love. She kissed Bob and he braced his legs as her thighs slid over his hips and her ankles crossed against the backs of his legs. He could smell her skin and feel the heat of her flesh and the tidal pull of each one of their organs and muscles hanging as if suspended beneath their separate skins. Tiana's mouth came away from Bob's and her lips grazed his ear.

"I will miss you when you leave tomorrow on your mission. How long will you be gone?"

"I should be back by Tuesday. Those two days away from you will seem like an eternity," Bob said.

When Bob left on his mission the following morning he could sense danger for her, but didn't know what to make of it. When he returned on Tuesday Nova informed him that someone had broken into Tiana's apartment on Sunday afternoon and killed her with a laser gun. Nothing was taken from her apartment and the police have no idea who killed her or why.

Since her body wasn't discovered until two days after her death, it was impossible to use quantum medicine to revive her. If her body had been found less than one hour after physical death, she could have been saved with the use of quantum medicine techniques.

Bob in all his 105 years had never met a woman he wanted to marry until Tiana came into his life. Since her death he had never seriously become involved with another woman and had no plans to do so.

His normal life was impossible in 2005. Bob is a resourceful agent and could always adapt to his new environment in different time periods. He began his day with a protein tablet dissolved in hot water and a mental review of Friday's events.

The introduction of Special Agent Michele Peterman to this assignment was at first viewed by Bob as an obstacle and interference. He quickly changed his mind about her and somewhat intuitively felt she could be of help to him. The TTSA did not routinely make itself known to the governments of different time periods. Bob normally was on his own. Having the resources of the FBI was indeed an advantage.

Trusting Michele Peterman's discretion was his only concern. Bob's instincts were nearly always correct and he trusted her. Besides, who would believe her if she attempted to blow his cover to her superiors?

His thoughts turned to Drax and Striker's alliance with the reptilian. Bob had his share of confrontations with cannibalistic and militant reptilians in the past. They were significant throughout the last several hundred thousand years of human development, always trying to enslave or exterminate our species. Many of his missions led him to direct conflict with reptilians from various time periods.

As a scholar he quickly reviewed the religious references to reptilians from his prior research. The Old Testament frequently refers to demons and devils as serpents who live within the Earth. The serpent of the Garden of Eden was known as Nachash. Many Hebrew scholars contend that this creature was a bipedal or hominid reptile of great intelligence.

It is also known through studies of evolution that the limbs of many reptile species atrophied over time, as the creatures lost the need for them. The Bible speaks of how the serpent from the garden was cursed to crawl upon its belly after its successful temptation of Eve, and eventually Adam, to eat the apple from the Tree of Knowledge. This implies that the infamous serpent of the garden walked upright!

In Numbers 21:6 of the Old Testament we read, "And the Lord sent fiery serpents among the people, and they bit the people, and much people of Israel died." The Nagas from ancient Indian mythology are described as humanoid lizards or serpents. From ancient texts over thousands of years old we find these Nagas ranked with gods, but later were demoted. When the gods withdrew from the affairs of man the Nagas retreated to great underground cities where they guard their privacy.

In Celtic mythology the appearance of serpents and dragons was always followed by strife and infertility. Last, in Gnostic texts we find these types of high powers: the High God, who is most powerful; Elohim, the male God and co-creator with his female partner; and Edem/Eden, the goddess associated with the Earth, half maiden and half serpent, who creates the cosmos with Elohim.

A little known fact concerning Hitler is that he was fond of drawing a reptilian humanoid and even tried to publish a book in 1909 about it. From his works, including *Mein Kampf*, he mentions a meeting with "supermen" in underground bases and that their eyes "were fierce and I was afraid."

Bob went to his holographic resonator to report in with Nova. He briefed her on Friday's events and awaited her response.

"OK hotshot, you now have an unauthorized FBI agent tagging along who is afraid to report an attempted murder and is patiently waiting for you to prove to her that you are a time traveler. Good work, Bob. How about enlisting the Girl Scouts next?" Nova commented sarcastically.

"Look, I know it doesn't sound good now, but I have a feeling she can be of great help. You know how accurate my intuition is."

"Yes, Merlin the Magnificent, I am aware of your track record. What do you need from me?"

"I would eternally appreciate two additional teleporter units, extra universal computer chips and thorough research on a football and baseball game."

Bob went into detail about the test he discussed with Michele concerning establishing evidence of his being a chrononaut. Nova patiently noted his request and supported his plan.

"I will throw in a news item to go along with the game details. Just don't go on CNN and announce yourself to the world. One FBI special agent in our confidence is more than enough."

"Thanks, Chief. I would greatly appreciate that info ASAP. Over and out," Bob countered Nova's earlier facetious remark.

Within an hour Bob received his equipment and a thorough report on Sunday's activities. He faxed Michele the results and spent the rest of the day testing his equipment and orienting himself to Los Angeles. Nova was able to provide Bob with the location of Striker's craft, now stored in one of Mannaco's warehouses and kept invisible by 36th-century technology. It is easy to trace any such crafts that originated in the 36th-century and has traveled back or forward to any time era.

Bob decided not to visit the warehouse yet. He quickly deduced that Striker brought back several other devices from the 36th-century and that would make him a worthy adversary. Nova's research also included supplemental data on Striker's background.

Mustafa Striker is half Egyptian and half German. He was thoroughly trained in the sciences and excelled in his university studies. Striker planned to be a chrononaut, but when he was rejected from the chrononaut academy chose the diplomatic route. His background was similar to chrononauts in that Striker knew hyperspace physics and the theory of time travel. If he wanted to cause trouble, he most likely was well versed in what to do.

Nova usually encourages Bob to make his own plans during a mission and this was no exception. It would be a simple matter to arrest Striker now, but what about Drax's plan? Bob needed to know precisely what that reptilian had in mind. Arresting Striker before destroying Drax's plan would be short-sided. Drax would undoubtedly enlist another ally to effect his plan. Patience was the key for now.

On Sunday morning Michele awoke with the sense that this was to be an unusual day. As the morning sun peeked its way into her bedroom's opened window, she immediately noticed the almost crystal clarity of the air. How long has it been, she thought, since she had seen a sky so clear and breathed air so fragrantly fresh?

She climbed out of bed and made her way into the kitchen. She fed Sheba, put on a pot of coffee and then dressed in a pair of sweats. She washed her face, brushed her teeth, poured a mug of coffee, and walked outside onto the lawn where the early birds were picking through the loot of her neighbor's garbage.

Today was to be the test of Bob's sports predictions. She also noted the news item he reported,

which she felt couldn't possibly be faked. This item
stated that at 10:12 A.M. Pacific Standard Time (PST)
one Farahad Bozin would be captured by the LAPD in a
high-speed chase ending in West Covina. Bozin will rob
a convenience store in Koreatown and shoot the owner in
the left arm.

On Saturday she ran a fingerprint check on Bob.
He had conveniently left very readable prints on his
coffee cup. Both the FBI's computer bank and that of
Interpol drew a blank. His fingerprints were simply not
on file anywhere. She mused to herself, how can his
prints be on file if he won't exist for 1,500 years?

As she settled herself comfortably on the couch,
Sheba jumped next to her and placed her feline body on
her favorite pillow. Michele decided to watch the
Dolphin/Jet football game at 10:00 A.M. The game
started at about 10:05 and Michele kept Bob's fax handy
on the coffee table.

By 11:00 A.M. she noted three scoring drives had
occurred and were precisely reported by Bob. Suddenly
the TV screen was overlaid with LATE BREAKING
NEWS.

A young Japanese newscaster appeared on a street
with three police cars in the background.

"This is Karen Yamamoto reporting from West
Covina, where a high-speed police chase just ended. At
10:12 this morning Farahad Bozin held up a 7/11 in
Koreatown and wounded the owner in the left arm with a
stolen gun. We will keep you apprised of this case as
time permits."

The color drained from Michele's face. How

could Bob have known these details? She decided to follow the rest of the Dolphin/Jet game and the Yankee game at 1:00 P.M.

Throughout the next five and a half hours Michele became enthralled with her two favorite sports. She only occasionally followed football and baseball, but this was a special circumstance. By 4:30 P.M. the Yankee game ended. Bob was correct on all scoring plays, in addition to the newscast.

A shadow of anxiety crossed her face. Could he really be from the future? She knew this topic could not be brought up to Assistant Director Drake Collins. As she expected, her telephone rang just as the game ended.

"Did you watch television today?" Bob asked.

"Yes, and you darn well know your predictions were perfect."

"Not predictions," Bob corrected her. "These were historical records sent by my superior from the 36th-century. Can we meet?"

"OK, you know where I live. C'mon over."

Bob decided to use a more conventional mode of transportation. He drove to Michele's apartment in a black 1985 Toyota MR2 that came with the house. He loved the flat black design that reminded him of a small 21st-century plane. He stocked CDs of the 1960s in the glove compartment and was on his way.

Michele greeted him at the front door with Sheba making her repeated purring sounds. Bob entered and noted a differently attired Michele Peterman than one would have seen earlier. She appeared as a poised, coolly attractive blond woman in white linen trousers, a pale blue silk shirt, flat-heeled shoes. Her ashy-blond hair, still damp from the shower, was brushed back neatly from her face. Her flawless cosmetic mask betrayed no sign of alarm, not even of special concern.

"You know that anyone in my field who testified to the accuracy of time travelers from the future would be completely ostracized and probably removed from active duty. So just who the hell are you?"

"My name is Bob Gullon and I function as a chrononaut, or time traveler, from the 36th-century. Mustafa Striker is a wanted man and has the capacity to cause many problems if he is not stopped."

"Just what are these problems?" Michele asked.

"I don't know yet. I'm hoping that together we can find out what he is up to."

"Then what? Who is going to arrest him, me or you?" Michele now seemed irritated.

"That, Special Agent Peterman, is to be determined. I trust you can see that I should be given priority. Let's not concern ourselves with that now."

"OK. What do you know about the FBI?"

"Well, your motto is fidelity, bravery and integrity and you have 50 field offices with over 400 satellite branches known as resident agencies. Special agents, such as yourself, oversee each field office, except for the largest field offices in Washington, D.C., New York and Los Angeles. They are headed by an assistant director. How am I doing so far?"

"Very good. Anything else?"

"The priorities of the FBI are to:

1. Protect the U.S. from terrorist attack.
2. Protect the U.S. against foreign intelligence operations and espionage.
3. Protect against cyber-based attacks and high technology crimes.
4. Combat public corruption at all levels.
5. Protect civil rights.
6. Combat transnational and national criminal organizations and enterprises.
7. Combat major white-collar crime.
8. Combat significant violent crimes.
9. Support federal, state, county, municipal, and international partners.
10. Upgrade technology to successfully perform the FBI's mission."

"OK, that's enough. Boy, you sure do your homework TTSA Bob Gullon."

"Please call me Bob. May I call you Michele?"

"Why not? Whenever I entertain someone from 1,500 years in the future I prefer to drop the usual formalities," Michele declared sarcastically.

"Very funny Michele. I have a colleague with a sense of humor. I sense that you want to know other things about my role here."

"Oh yeah! Are you just a futuristic cop, or what?" Michele asked.

"We chrononauts are much more than that. Our main function is to assist others in their spiritual growth, along with guiding them technologically and providing protection."

"Just how do you affect the spiritual growth of these people?"

"Interestingly enough, one of the ways we do that is through automatic writing. Throughout history there have been many examples of automatic writing leading to a compilation of previously unknown knowledge that often surpasses the level of humanity's learning at the time it is written.

"We can look to the origin of religious scriptures, especially the Koran, that was the result of direct 'angelic' communication. The Theosophical movement, the Mystery Schools, Free Masonry, the Rosicrucians, the writings of Thomas Jefferson, Rousseau, Leonardo Da Vinci, Thomas Edison, Benjamin Franklin, and a host of others suggest something beyond normal acquisition of knowledge."

Michele did not have much of a social life. She rarely dated and found it impossible to attract a man into her life who could relate to dating a dedicated FBI agent with strong spiritual interests. Men were either too judgmental and dismissive or too unstable and "airy fairy."

The conversation became directed to a discussion of soulmates.

"So what do 36th-century people think about soulmates? Do you believe in them?"

"I can speak for more than just my personal beliefs. We all believe in karma and reincarnation. Yes, we do believe in soulmates and the principle of relationships functioning as part of the ascension process."

"Tell me more," Michele now leaned forward in her chair and expressed her undivided attention.

"The ultimate soulmate is a 'twin flame.' Many eons ago each human soul was part of an energy complex and perfectly balanced in positive and negative polarity. We would refer to these as masculine and feminine traits. For whatever reason a devolution took place and each soul energy complex separated itself into individual entities who reincarnate periodically as either male or female biological beings.

"This is fascinating and fits in with what I have read. Please go on."

"The original source of this soul energy is what we call the god energy complex, which is perfect. Each masculine and feminine soul energy complex temporarily forgot its oneness with the god energy complex, lost its perfect energy status and began a process of devolution that has resulted in our dysfunctional behavior today. However, these twin souls each seek one another to reunite not only with themselves, but with the god energy complex, thus regaining their perfect energy status. At this point they no longer reincarnate, but can function as spirit guides assisting others in the ascension process, or ascend themselves."

"You don't seem to have a high opinion of 21st-century humankind, do you?"

"I am only reporting what I observe and what history teaches me. Your society is dominated by fear and anxiety. A universal fear of violent crime, the actions of strangers and terrorism predominate. Yet, most people are more likely to be injured in car accidents or household negligence than to be raped, robbed or murdered. Just about half of all serious crimes are never reported, mostly because these victims expect no help from overburdened police. Even when the police do their job, their work is undermined by clogged courts and punitive prisons that breed more crime."

"But don't you have similar problems in your century? Look at Striker's actions," Michele countered.

"Striker is a rare exception. Your world is divided, not united, and can't seem to cooperate enough to resolve major social problems. People can behave only in terms of how they perceive themselves and the world about them. And these perceptions are completely determined by one's beliefs of philosophy of life.

In addition, your world is characterized by dedicating your major national energies and resources to war and paranoid preparations for war. If you had devoted the same amount of money and national effort to solving your social problems that you did to waging your various wars, you could have ended the poverty cycle forever and gone a long way toward resolving many of your nation's other social problems. Even your welfare system is so politically corrupt and inadequate that it not only ignored the worst cases of human neglect and poverty, but actually perpetuated poverty and ignorance from one generation to the next. We have no such system in the 36th-century."

"So are you saying that your century is characterized by a more spiritually based society?"

"Yes, exactly. Most of us believe that every cell responds to our every thought, thereby making us that which we believe ourselves to be. We know that we are not the victims of circumstances, but rather the designers of our own destiny, the creators of our own reality. We know that this life holds only those experiences which we chose for our own growth."

"But why would a soul choose a devolution path?"

"Every soul has a choice. It's called free will. We are always responsible for our actions. When any individual starts caring about others—when he starts breaking down the barriers of prejudice and fear that separate men from each other, he then realizes that he lived many lives as he devolved down a continuum of awareness toward amnesia, or less awareness. He then begins his evolutionary trip back toward even greater awareness of his oneness with the god energy complex heading to ascension."

For a few minutes Michele pondered what Bob was saying, as she gazed out of the window overlooking a dead-end street. She then turned to Bob and continued her questioning.

"Bob, who does your society respect the most?"

"Contrary to your time in which entertainers and athletes achieve what you consider to be the most valuable rewards of fame and money, we place our tutors in the position of most respected and admired."

"What do you mean by tutors?"

"Our education is rarely the classroom format you are used to. Most of our population is educated by specially trained tutors. By the time our citizens reach what you would call adolescence, they see their tutor only once a week. We are all motivated to do self-learning."

"That is quite different from our current system," Michele commented.

"The reason is actually quite simple. Your lives are so miserable and unfulfilled that you utilize any sort of entertainment (and drugs) to escape. Naturally, entertainers and athletes would be paid more than anyone else."

"That doesn't say much for the value we place on education, does it? Teaching is one of our lowest-paid professions," Michele admitted.

"Your educational system is characterized by inadequately prepared teachers who are expected to teach their students how to memorize facts and detail instead of how to think creatively. Much time is spent on subjects which are of little use to the average person, while most learning programs give little or no attention to the most important subject of all—human behavior and life philosophy, including spiritual growth."

"Getting back to Striker, I hear he is working on antigravity technology. What do you know about that field?" she asked.

"We know that Mannaco is using nano-gold and monatomic element technology. Antigravity applications are also theorized from monatomic elements. Monatomic elements are operative high-temperature superconductors, and levitation is a consequence of this activity. Boeing is working on Project Grasp at its top-secret Phantom Works in Seattle, while Project Greenglow is its equivalent in Great Britain. The U.S. and British have a joint venture in this field called Project

Falcon. In August of 2003 British Aerospace and Boeing met at the Pentagon to discuss plans for a 6,000-mile-per-hour aircraft. This is five times the speed of the former Concorde."

"But just how can he achieve antigravity?" she wondered.

"There are three ways to achieve antigravity. Providing a force opposing gravity is one method. Magnetic or electrostatic repulsion is an example. Second, finding a new force that repels gravity would do the trick. This force has as of yet not been discovered.

"Turning gravity against itself is the third way. Einstein's theory of relativity allows for such a force. Such a universal repulsive force is theorized to have existed immediately following the Big Bang. Our early universe supposedly grew enormously due to this repulsive force. Such repulsive forces also exist near the event horizons of some black holes."

"This is fascinating," Michele commented. "What commercial applications do you suspect Mannaco could do with this technique?"

"Antigravity has enormous applications. Consider:

- Floating oil tankers from continent to continent a few inches above water to reduce oil spills.
- Floating bicycles.
- Floating cars.
- Floating ships.
- Floating railway trains.
- Floating airplanes.

- Floating spacecraft.
- New types of ski lifts.
- Much more rapid building and construction through antigravity cranes and perhaps fields to hold up the whole building.
- Cities floating over marshland, water or high in the air.
- Making rivers run uphill to irrigate parched areas or deserts.
- Raising the Titanic or other wrecked ships.
- New recreation areas and sports allowing man-powered flights.
- Less damage to the ozone layer of the atmosphere due to the elimination of burning large quantities of chemical fuel to raise and fly planes.

"Last, interdimensional travel is another possible result of monatomic elements. Hal Puthoff, the director of the Institute for Advanced Studies in Austin, Texas, authored "Gravity As a Zero-point Fluctuation Force" in the March 1, 1989, issue of *Physical Review Letters*. He stated that when particles begin to resonate in two dimensions, they lose four-ninths of their weight. With increased heating the weight would reduce to absolute zero and would disappear. They would return to a visible state upon subsequent cooling. We now know that it is possible to transport matter into other dimensions and return them to ours. My teleporting back in time is an extreme example of this possibility."

Bob immediately realized that Striker must have powerful political connections. All Bob had to do was recall what happened to John Searl. John Roy Robert Searl was born on May 2, 1932, in England. His work has led to quantum leaps in our understanding and application of antigravity research and functioning devices. He was victimized by both the scientific establishment and his own government.

When he was just fourteen, Searl constructed his first Search Effect Generator (SEG). This project was financed by George Hines and the six SEGs produced were all lost. The problem with these devices is that as they speeded up, they produced an energy field that resulted in their losing their gravity. Since Searl couldn't contain his field, these SEGS rose up into the atmosphere and never returned.

From 1946 to 1961 a total of 41 of these levity discs were built, tested and flown. The British government raided Searl's lab during the 1960s and 1970s, confiscated these discs and destroyed his notes. The Southern Electricity Board prosecuted and imprisoned him for stealing electricity!

The mechanism of Searl's "levity discs" was based on the principle of a segmented metal disc creating free electrons within the iron surface to be spun off by centrifugal force. These electrons are collected at the periphery of the discs and in some way creates an antigravity effect. Conventional electromagnets could then be placed uniformly around the periphery of the disc, converting the free electrons into a useful electromagnetic force (EMT).

The disc's iron surface was segmented to provide a pulsed electron flow. Multiple electromagnets created a very high pulsed EMF flow with this design.

When these discs were tested electricity was produced at a rather high wattage level. Static electricity and the smell of ozone were noted by observers as the disc attained higher speeds. It rose to a height of fifty feet during demonstrations.

In Striker's warehouse, located in a seedy part of downtown Los Angeles, four crime bosses were getting ready to leave. They had just held a meeting with Striker reviewing the money-laundering Striker's various companies had completed with their criminal organizations.

These men were Fabrizio Romano of Detroit, Vincenze Bellani from Chicago, Pasquale DeNardo from New York and Lorenzo Giamona from Miami. This money-laundering activity was Striker's payoff for murders they had committed to eliminate his enemies. The icing on the cake was that Striker made a considerable profit on each transaction. According to Striker's megalomaniac perspective, life was very good indeed.

"Hey Bob, all this talk is making me hungry. Can I talk you into having dinner here?"

"Sure. I welcome any change to my usual fare of burgers and fries."

It was a leisurely meal with lots of laughing and talking, and Bob had an opportunity to appreciate the remarkable intelligence, broad knowledge and varied interests. He also had the opportunity to try some strange new foods that he found delicious, but didn't ask what they were made of. He would enjoy the meal more if he was not forced to consider the content of the food he was eating. These concerns didn't last long.

After they finished eating, Michele cleared the table and Bob followed her to the kitchen with his plate.

"You don't need to do that. After all, you are my guest. Why don't you go and have a seat on the couch. I will join you in a few minutes," she said.

Bob settled in on the couch, but his evening was cut short by a flash from his pen-like pager.

"I'm sorry to leave like this, but Nova is trying to communicate with me and I need to return to Woodland Hills. I'll contact you tomorrow morning. Good night."

Michele understood. It had been a long day. As she scanned around the place, the sight of her small but cozy apartment on the ground floor of an old two-story building in Brentwood always eased the tension that had been building up all day. She plopped onto her couch, pulled off her shoes, and stretched her aching feet out onto the ancient coffee table as her cat, Sheba, jumped up to join her.

Michele wasn't aware of the small computer chip tracking device that Bob placed in her purse. Just five minutes after Bob left, a thick-necked man of forty-six who perspired easily, with heavy-lidded frog's eyes and a damp, hungry smile checked his watch. He wore an electric-blue crinkled-cotton shirt, checkered polyester trousers creased at the thighs, and a "Navajo" leather belt with a flashy brass buckle. A black onyx ring was on his right hand embedded in fatty flesh. He looked like someone on vacation. In fact, this was Otto Schmidt's typical attire for a Sunday evening. Otto was still living in the 1970s.

The next thing Michele knew was that her door was broken down by an angry polyester brute who quickly flashed his shiny Walther PPK gun at her and ordered her to come with him in his black sedan.

Five

A collection of cold, modern low-rise buildings surrounded one of Mannaco's smaller warehouses located in a semi-seedy part of downtown Los Angeles. A bus passed by the old building in need of a serious paint job. A black sedan approached out of the distance.

Inside the car Michele and Otto stared defiantly at each other. As they approached the warehouse driveway, a guard in a wooden kiosk waved them through. They finally arrived at the main entrance of the building and Otto ordered Michele out of the car. She got out of the car and slammed the door shut.

Otto led her inside the building and beyond the mostly empty main section of the warehouse. Michele thought it odd that such a successful company as Mannaco would have a near empty warehouse. She would shortly have her curiosity satisfied.

Beyond the main warehouse Michele was led through a winding series of corridors to an examination room. She noted an observation booth adjacent to this room separated by a glass divider.

Seated at the control panel, which resembled a switcher from a recording studio, was Alfred Doyle. A row of video monitors occupied much of this space. Some of these monitors functioned as security devices, while two focused in on the examination room chair.

Michele was immediately strapped into a large chair and given an injection of Valium. Otto assumed a protective stance by the door, as Doyle began with his instructions.

"Special Agent Peterman: You are sitting in a chair that provides us an electro-molecular connection to all your memories and physical data on your body right down to the sub-atomic level. We call this the alpha neuro imager (ANI). My name is Alfred Doyle and I will be your guide," Doyle stated sarcastically.

"What is it you want to know, Doyle?" Michele's speech was starting to slur.

"Everything you know about Mannaco and Dr. Striker."

"Why don't you just ask me?"

"Ah, we are not that stupid," countered Doyle.

Alfred Doyle was a thin, muscular man in his twenties who was known for his complete lack of a sense of humor and his tendency to alienate everyone in his presence. He was one hundred percent British and proud of it.

"In a few moments we will be able to see what

you're thinking. My friend Otto, here, will also be able to see your thoughts from monitor 6."

Several of the monitors functioning as security screens scanned the corridors and main entrance. One monitor was filled with static, while the final one showed Michele still struggling somewhat.

"The bitch is fighting it, Doyle," barked Otto.

"That won't last long," Doyle countered.

Doyle now turned on the microphone and began speaking softly to Michele.

"Okay, Michele, I want you to look at the screen in front of you," ordered Doyle.

Michele looked up at a video monitor displaying a series of hypnotic star bursts shortly followed by ever-expanding and evolving geometric patterns. The room was filled with soothing resonant sounds that seemed to cause her whole mind and body to resonate in similarly evolving and enlarging patterns.

"Relax. You're in a completely safe place with friends that care about you," cooed Doyle. His voice is soothing and relaxing, as if he'd done this a thousand times before.

"Bullshit," Michele blurted out.

At first she was leery and tried to resist the strange sensations caused by the incredible visual and audible stimuli. Michele fought to keep her eyes open and her mind in control. It soon proved to be a futile attempt.

"There is no point in fighting, Michele. You can feel your resistance weakening, fading into the distance."

Michele's eyes started getting heavier and heavier. Finally she gave up all resistance and found herself flowing on a gentle river of multiple sensations until she seemed to enter an infinite ocean of unspeakable unity, oneness, and balance accompanied by the most soul-satisfying feeling of harmony imaginable.

"Good, Michele. That's right. Relax. You'll be our tour guide on this great journey into your mind."

Doyle's attention was drawn to the monitors starting to show static-filled flashes of random scenes from her mind: meeting with Drake Collins, playing with Sheba, jogging at Venice beach, a trip to Catalina Island, etc.

Michele's breathing was steady and calm.

"Now tell us all you know about Mannaco and Dr. Mustafa Striker."

Michele fought the instructions. Otto and Doyle were watching as their equipment records what was going on in Michele's mind.

"Please, Michele, do what I ask."

Michele didn't respond and now began to struggle. Doyle got quickly annoyed and stimulated her brain with the press of a button sending a laser beam to her right temporal lobe. Michele screamed and went unconscious.

Now the video monitor showed nothing but static. Michele awakened shortly and the images continued. The screen depicted her reviewing the FBI's files on Striker and Mannaco. After several inconsequential images, her talks with Bob Gullon were depicted.

Just then Striker entered the observation booth and pounded his fist on the table.

"Damn that TTSA Gullon. Damn the government. Why don't they just leave me alone?" Striker barked.

"What do you want me to do, sir?" Doyle asked.

"Ask her what Gullon knows about me."

The next several scenes depicted parts of Michele and Bob's earlier conversation and the lifesaving incident at Mannaco's lab. She then again lost consciousness.

"Oh, great. That freak is the one who froze me on Friday. I'm gonna kill that bastard!" Otto threatened.

"One thing at a time, my dear German. We need to get hold of him first," Striker stated as he weighed his options.

Striker immediately removed the videotapes and used his thought wave scrambler to delete all references to the 36th-century from Doyle and Otto's brains. It was not prudent to let his agents know his true identity, as Striker had enough problems to deal with now. Having a fellow 36th-century citizen, and a chrononaut at that, chasing him put a damper on everything he planned.

When he arrived in Los Angeles in 1999 Striker bought the warehouse to first hide his flying saucer that brought him back in time, along with Taatos' equipment. He used an invisibility shield to hide the craft and began to set up Taatos' equipment known as a wormhole linear accelerator (WLA).

The WLA functioned as a superconductor and when exotic matter was applied to the wormhole it created, Striker was able to travel back to 1999. His plan now was rather simple. All he had to do was create a dozen new wormholes and not apply exotic matter. This would cause severe tears in the fabric of space-time and by the 36th-century an uncontrollable black hole would be generated. This singularity would destroy our galaxy.

The best laid plans of mice and men often go astray, it is said. Since Striker was not that familiar with Taatos' equipment, he failed to place the exotic matter in one key location of the wormhole. This destroyed a computer chip critical to the function of the WLA. The result was that Striker was prevented from creating wormholes. Not only could he not accomplish his mission, but he also could not travel back or forward in time. He was stuck in 2005!

To make the most out of his situation, Striker forgot about his agreement with Drax and concentrated on accumulating as much money and power as he could. He had become a true paranoid megalomaniac. The presence of Bob Gullon now ruined his plan. He now knew that either Bob or the FBI will arrest him eventually.

Making billions of dollars is not easy. Striker made connections with various criminal organizations in order to get his technology accepted by the U.S. In return Striker became part of money laundering schemes to pay back his criminal confederates and make even more money through the exchange of funds. Striker charged his clients a hefty fee each time they laundered their drug dealing funds through one of his legitimate enterprises. With a little diligent research the FBI could make a serious case against Striker and Mannaco. Michele and Gullon had to be stopped at any cost.

Bob arrived at his Woodland Hills home a little tired but excited about this mission. He found Michele Peterman to be an interesting woman. A sense of attraction was most definitely evident, but something prevented this from being sexual. He didn't know what it was and decided to communicate with Nova.

Bob briefed Nova and was advised to proceed with caution. Nova had reservations about Michele's role in this mission and was concerned that she might, at the last minute, end up arresting Striker. Bob assured Nova that these concerns were unnecessary. He informed his superior that even if Michele attempted that deception, his skills and technological weaponry could easily place Striker in his hands.

As Bob turned on his locator unit he was shocked to see that Michele was not at home. Instead, his gadget informed him that she was in one of Striker's warehouses. This was not only odd, it meant trouble.

He could think of only two possible reasons for this. Either she decided to snoop around this warehouse by herself late on a Sunday evening, or she was now Striker's prisoner. Bob voted for the latter and drove to the warehouse.

As he approached the warehouse he quickly noted the security cameras and the guard's kiosk. Bob decided to park the MR2 a block away from the warehouse and activate his morphologic cell regulator (MCR), which rendered him invisible. He now walked comfortably past the guard, who he thought was of Latin origin due to the slicked-back hair. Upon close inspection, Bob observed that the guard's hair appeared shellacked, almost metallic.

Bob entered the warehouse in his now invisible state by merely passing through the locked door. He was in the fifth dimension and could pass through any physical barrier. In order to effect any action on our three-dimensional world, he must slow down his frequency vibrational rate and reappear.

Using the television monitors as his guide, he quickly located Michele. He decided to remain invisible and observe.

"The subject is not going to provide additional information, Dr. Striker. What do you want me to do?" Doyle asked.

"Kill the bitch," ordered Otto.

"I concur with my security chief. She is no longer useful and I suspect we can expect a visit from her friend at any moment," replied Striker.

With that last remark Bob turned off his MCR and reappeared. He quickly placed Otto and Doyle in suspended animation. Striker pointed a phaser weapon at Michele and confronted Bob.

"You have interfered with my work for the last time. Make one false move and I will kill your girlfriend. Now lay down your weapons and step back," demanded Striker. The fury of his outburst cooled slightly, but his order still held a brittle edge.

Bob had no choice but to follow Striker's orders. He placed his various weapons on the floor in front of him and stepped back six feet.

"You forgot to include your teleporter. Slide it over now."

Bob did as he was instructed and waited for Striker's next move. Striker pocketed the teleporter immediately.

"You know this is rather amusing. Here I am stuck

in the 21st-century unable to leave to go back or forward in time, and you provide me with the solution," bragged Striker.

"What do you mean?" Bob inquired.

"You see, before I kill you I am going to reveal my purpose in coming here," Striker responded.

Just then Michele regained consciousness and winked at Bob. She was now positioned behind Striker and if there were only some way she could free herself, both of them could be saved.

"My goal was to use the WLA to create a wormhole and not line it with exotic matter. Do you know what would then take place?"

"Not much now, but the tear resulting in the fabric in space-time could lead to dire consequences in the future," Bob answered.

"Exactly. Consider the creation of an uncontrollable black hole that would suck up everything in its path," Striker retorted.

"But that would destroy the Earth and probably a good part of the galaxy, including you!"

"Not if I'm not here," gloated Striker.

"Ah, it now becomes crystal clear. You made a pact with the Devil in the form of Drax, didn't you?" Bob deduced.

"Most certainly. You are looking at the next leader of a planet of humans in a far galaxy."

"Do you actually think that reptilian maniac is going to keep his promise? Even if you accomplish your goal, what does he need you for? He will just eliminate you as he has done to thousands of other short-sighted power-crazed fools."

With that last remark Striker pounded his fist into the desk adjacent to him and aimed his lethal phaser at Bob. Bob quickly ran for his phaser and expertly aimed it at the straps holding Michele to the ANI. She now freed herself and tackled Striker.

Striker threw Michele to one side and ran into a distant corridor. Bob quickly retrieved his MCR and other weapons and checked on Michele. He was suddenly jumped from behind by the guard he observed before in the kiosk. All of this commotion attracted the guard's attention.

Bob and the guard struggled when Bob kneed the guard in the groin and then slammed his fist against the guard's nose. Michele grabbed for her purse located by the control panel and reached for her gun. It's not there!

As Bob and Michele began to leave, the guard scrambled to his feet and leaped at Bob, catching him by the ankle. Michele rendered a karate chop to the back of the guard's head and this rendered the guard unconscious. Bob and Michele ran out of the warehouse, heading for the MR2.

Leaving the building, Bob told Michele that the MR2 was parked a block away and they should run to get there as soon as possible. She informed him that the effects of the Valium have worn off enough for her to move quickly.

Suddenly, two Mexican gangbangers stepped out of a walkway in the alley adjacent to the warehouse.

"Hey, man. What is your hurry? You lost?" gangbanger #1 laughed.

"No, we're just fine. Have a nice evening," Bob responded.

"No, seriously. We help you, good," gangbanger #2 replied.

Suddenly, they grabbed Bob and in the momentary confusion Michele karate chopped gangbanger #1, who grabbed Bob from behind. Bob kicked gangbanger #2 in the groin and watched as gangbanger #2 buckled over.

Gangbanger #1 tried to help out his friend, still struggling to get to his feet. Bob managed to grab the arm of gangbanger #1 to swing him around, forcing his body to slam into that of gangbanger #2, causing him to lose consciousness. Bob shoved gangbanger #1 aside. He grabbed Michele by the arm and they fled to the MR2.

Gangbanger #1 got up and began to run toward the MR2 in pursuit of Bob and Michele with his knife in his right hand. There's a momentary bloodcurdling scream as gangbanger #1 was hit by Otto's black sedan, his body thrown ten feet away by the impact.

Alfred Doyle was driving the black sedan with nobody else in the car. Otto was still groggy and Striker was just plain pissed off. Bob saw a trail of oil from old parked cars with leaky engines and fired his phaser at the puddle of oil closest to these cars. A flame shot out and followed the trail of oil igniting one parked car after the next. KABOOM! KABOOM! KABOOM! The parked cars leading up to the black sedan exploded in a fiery chain reaction. Doyle was engulfed in flames and let out a bloodcurdling scream. KABOOM!! The black sedan exploded, killing Doyle.

Striker and Otto watched as this scene unfolded and shook their heads.

"I'm surrounded by incompetence," barked Striker. Otto didn't know what to say.

Bob got behind the wheel of the MR2 and Michele took the passenger seat. They were both dirty and exhausted, resembling a homeless couple more than they did government agents.

"Whereto Bob?" asked Michele.

"Let's go to your apartment and find a temporary home for Sheba. You need a change of address pronto."

Upon arriving at Michele's apartment she called one of her neighbors who readily agreed to take Sheba in and look after her for a while. Michele quickly packed some clothes and they drove to Bob's Woodland Hills home.

"You'll be safer here. Why don't you shower and change clothes while I notify my superior about tonight's events?"

With that Michele went into the guest room and used the adjacent shower. Bob went into his office and prepared to contact Nova. First, he emptied his pockets to reorganize his weapons and noted that he had an extra hologram resonator chip that wasn't his. It must have come from Striker's pocket. Bob inserted it into his hologram resonator and played the message.

Before his eyes he could see Drax alone and in an angry mood. Drax stated:

YOUR INCOMPETENCE IS STAGGERING. SINCE YOU CAN'T OPERATE YOUR WLA, FIND A WAY TO GO BACK FURTHER IN TIME AND

CREATE RIPPLE POINTS, OR I WILL SEE TO IT
THAT YOU ARE KILLED. DO I MAKE MYSELF
CLEAR?

Bob knew all too well what this meant. Striker
now had his teleporter and could travel anywhere back in
time to change events in history. This would create large
tears in the fabric of space-time and these ripple points
would in turn create paradoxes. If enough of these ripple
points occurred, an uncontrollable black hole would be
generated and the entire universe could easily be
destroyed. One of the goals of chrononauts is to prevent
these ripple points from being generated.

"Don't you ever sleep, hot shot?" Nova asked.

"Listen chief, we have a big problem. Striker has
obtained one of my teleporters and has made a deal with
our old friend Drax to create ripple points to do you
know what."

"Just how did that little event transpire? No, never
mind the details. I will be sending you additional
teleporters, phasers and many extra computer chips to
record each of these communications."

"Why the extra computer chips, Nova?"

"Because if he is successful, paradoxes will change
everything and I won't be aware of what is happening.
We need this record to have our agency work properly
and for future incidents like this."

"Just how many ripple points need to be created to
generate the black hole?" Bob asked.

"That depends on just how serious the ripple point
is. I can calculate the precise effect once you inform me
as to the event. Obviously, it is more important to

prevent a ripple point, rather than to attempt to patch the resulting tears in the fabric of space-time."

Bob went on to review other events, including Michele's activities, and then signed off. Michele knocked on his door and wondered what their next move was going to be.

"Striker has a teleporter and can go back in time to any era. Fortunately, the unit has a tracer so I will know exactly when and where he goes."

"I just saw a box materialize on that weird machine in the other office. Anything I should know?" she asked.

"It's just some extra equipment I will need. Look, it's late and we have both been through hell. You can sleep in the guest room and tomorrow we will begin a new plan."

As Michele went off to bed Bob couldn't stop thinking about her. Hers was not the shallow, brittle beauty of a Hollywood starlet, but a deep almost spiritual essence that seemed to radiate from her. While her physical beauty was obvious, it was the sparkling multifaceted depths of her mind that aroused and excited him with a completeness that was unknown to him in previous relationships.

Bob considered his options and suddenly felt Michele's tremendous strength of patience, understanding, courage and spirituality. He had been both mentally and physically bombarded by the very power of her being.

Frustration suddenly entered Bob's awareness. In addition to being against a dozen rules he could think of, becoming romantically involved with Michele seemed to be blocked by an outside force. He couldn't place his finger on it, but something was saying to him discipline, discipline, discipline. With that he took a shower and went to bed.

Michele could not fall asleep in the guest room. Her thoughts were dominated, not so much by the activities of the day, but by Bob Gullon. She was very drawn to this mystery man. It had been over six months since she had had a real date.

She now mentally reviewed the only lovers she had known. There was John in college. A Henry while she was at the FBI academy, then two years with Hal and six months with Neal. Only four men in her whole life.

Now her thoughts returned to Bob. She is suddenly more aware of his body. His gentle but undeniable vitality, courage, intelligence, resourcefulness and spirituality now dominated her thoughts. She was puzzling over her emotions: It was as if she didn't want to admit that she cared greatly for Bob. Finally, she drifted off to sleep.

Michele quickly dreamed that she was in a rustic inn of some kind sitting at a table with Bob. From behind the bar, a fat, dark waiter looked over at them. When they'd come in, he hadn't exactly greeted them with open arms. The only other lunchers were three men in the booth at the far end. They were hunched over platters of spaghetti, each one guarding his food as if afraid someone would steal it.

The waiter came out like a man with a mission, bearing plates heaped with meat. He brought them to the three men at the back, bowed, and served. Michele noted the musty odor and worn lace curtains drawn back carelessly from flyspecked windows, dark, dingy wood varnished so many times it looked like plastic. The booths that lined the mustard-colored walls were cracked black leather, the tables covered with checkered oilcloth.

Suddenly, Striker and Otto appeared with machine guns aimed at both of them. Bob whipped out his phaser and cut them down before either could pull their triggers.

Michele quickly entered into a second dream. This time she was in a futuristic home walking down a long, glass-enclosed outer hall. It was lighted both by the outside sunshine and by overhead lighting that seemed to radiate equally from all parts of the ceiling. She then turned down an interior hallway and was now standing before a large blue door.

When she opened this door she entered a beautifully decorated futuristic bedroom. Bob took her hand in his and touched her cheek firmly but gently. Immediately there was total silence. Michele did not feel uncomfortable and returned his look with confidence and a powerful feeling of contentment.

She joined Bob on the bed and both of them disrobed. Now she could hear sixties music in the background. They lay next to each other and touched each other's fingertips saying nothing. They did not move but each felt exquisite joy that kept mounting in intensity until the experience of each one was that of a mighty river.

The two great rivers shortly united as one. When the now joined river crested into one huge, tumultuous wave, they held each other tightly and moaned in ecstasy.

Their sounds gently receded in volume and intensity until the room was at last silent once more.

Michele awakened almost in a panic. The alarm clock read 2:25 A.M. She couldn't believe she had a sexual dream involving Bob. A wave of guilt ran over her. She was most definitely attracted to him, but felt it was wrong, very wrong. She fell back asleep and drifted into a peaceful rest.

Six

Synchronistically, Bob and Michele awoke in their separate beds at the same time. It was now Monday morning and their respective alarm clocks read 7:55 A.M. In the light of early morning an eerie calm prevailed. The morning sun was emerging out of a pearl-opalescent darkness of massed clouds, a fiery all-seeing eye.

They had both slept later than their usual time due to Sunday's activities. Michele greeted Bob in the kitchen as he boiled water for his protein drink. She found some coffee and brewed it. They exchanged a few words and Michele excused herself for half an hour to do some running. Running had always seemed to her the ultimate in physical freedom. Fortunately, sweats and running shoes were packed the previous evening.

When she returned, Bob had prepared a briefing

for her. He agreed to delay it until he answered a few of her questions.

"Can you tell me in plain English just how time travelers can affect our time and manipulate events?" she asked.

"Sure. First consider time as the fourth dimension of the space-time continuum. Scientists label this as a worm line. This worm line is a space-time line that stretches from the Big Bang (the creation of our universe) to the time the universe ceases to exist.

"A time traveler residing in the fifth dimension of hyperspace can manipulate the fourth dimension (time) and subsequently our easily observed three-dimensional universe in a manner similar to how a record player operates. Our three dimensions are guided by time very much like the way in which a record player's needle is guided by the grooves on the record's surface.

"Our time traveler can easily see your worm line just as you can see a two-dimensional character in a cartoon strip. If a three-dimensional object were to fall into this two-dimensional cartoon strip, the cartoon character would only see shapes appearing and disappearing. We, on the other hand, can view the entire scene simply by existing in our three-dimensional world.

"The universe is made up of an infinite number of worm lines. A time traveler can manipulate our worm line without our being aware of the process. Every dimension is connected to ours in some way and a time traveler can easily alter events in our past, present or future."

"But from what I heard yesterday, doesn't that

cause problems by creating ripple points or tears in the fabric of space-time?" she asked.

"It depends on the quality of the manipulation. The more you alter history from our present perception, the larger and more severe the tear. Most minor changes leave no lasting effects. Even the major ones can be patched by special equipment," Bob responded.

"Bob, can you give an example of how one of your time travelers affected our technology but avoided creating a major ripple point?"

"The best example I can think of is the RCA FRR 24 receiver. During the 1980s we sent this FRR 24 radio receiver back in time to 1933 to RCA's Rocky Point laboratory for disassembly and study.

"RCA analyzed its function and applied it to radios it manufactured. There was nothing else like this receiver at that time. Radio technology underwent major progress during 1933 and 1934 due to this receiver. To respond to your query, this resulted in only a minor tear in the fabric of space-time."

"Thanks. I actually think I understand this concept. It appears that reading several books on quantum mechanics and superstring theory has finally paid off."

Bob then began a long briefing during which he gave Michele a teleporter and instructed her to its use. He informed her that the red dot on the top left corner referred to a biochip he had implanted in his neck and as long as the red light was on, he was alive. If he were killed it would immediately go out.

Next on his list was the holographic resonator. He

showed Michele how to receive and send signals and how to store all messages and transmissions on special computer chips.

He then gave her a phaser gun and showed her its two functions, stun and kill. She appeared to absorb all of this technical data quickly and demonstrated to Bob successful use of each device.

"Do I get to use that luminous red ball thingy to freeze people?"

"No, not at this time. The reason I gave you the phaser is because you keep losing your gun," Bob related as he laughed.

Michele checked her purse and remembered that Otto had relieved her of her gun when he kidnapped her and brought her to Mannaco's warehouse on Sunday.

"What are our plans now, Bob?"

"I am waiting for Striker to make his move to a different time era. I don't know where he is now because he has become a timeliner."

"What in God's name is a timeliner?"

"Timeliners are those who remain in the same time era for five years or longer. They can move around geographically, but if they don't travel back or forward in time we cannot trace them with our teleporter and must wait for them to change time eras in order to track them."

"Does Striker know about this?"

"I suspect he doesn't. This is part of more recent and top secret chrononaut research and no ambassador would have access to that information."

Michele felt a sense of relief as Bob continued with his briefing.

"Now there is something I must tell you that may very well upset you."

"Go ahead. I'm all ears."

"On Friday I placed a small tracking device in your purse to keep tabs on you. That's how I knew you were in Mannaco's warehouse last night."

"Don't expect me to be angry. You saved my life, again, I might add, because of that."

"The reason I bring this up now is that I would like your permission to implant a small biochip in your neck, like the one I have, so me and my agency can keep track of you."

"What would be involved? Is this major surgery?"

"Heavens no. I simply run a small vibrator-like device along the back of your neck for about thirty seconds and it is implanted and registered simultaneously with me and the agency. Absolutely no pain or bleeding is involved."

"Don't you first have to let Nova know what you're doing?"

"I've already cleared this with her and she has prepared a file on you."

"Pretty sure of yourself, aren't you? You knew I would agree. Oh, all right, do your little vibrator thing."

Bob initiated the procedure and Michele giggled as he ran the device along the back of her neck.

"Now what do I do while you wait for Striker to be beamed back to another time?"

"This isn't Star Trek; nobody is going to sparkle out of the 21st-century. Remember, all we do is enter into the fabric of space-time."

"Please accept my apologies. So what about me?"

"I want you to remain here and use my home and/or your office to gather evidence for money-laundering and murder on Striker, Otto Schmidt and perhaps his CFO."

"Is that all you think is involved?"

"Yes. There might be a board member or two, but I doubt it."

"Why don't we just put Mannaco out of business once and for all?"

"You can, of course, but I wouldn't do it. That company is too important in its research and technology. A change at the top is indicated, but not its total destruction."

"But since the technology came from Striker, why is Mannaco so important?"

"He may have given them the nano-gold and monatomic technology, but now a competent team of researchers are developing this work. A long and tedious legal fight could seriously delay the application of that technology and that alone could create a serious ripple point."

Michele now understood Bob's strategy. In her mind she imagined trying to explain this to the melodramatic Assistant Director Drake Collins. The sound of laughter and anger following it would deafen anyone on the fourth floor of the Federal Building where their offices were located.

In his luxurious home in Calabasas, Mustafa Striker was one angry man. He now had to go back to several time eras and create ripple points to achieve his goal. All this could have been avoided if the WLA would simply work. Striker, in a sudden fit of rage, loudly swore as he slammed his fist onto his expensive mahogany desk in his study.

He was also angry that the very craft he used to come to the 21st-century was teleported back to Taatos' laboratory by that thorn in his side, Bob Gullon. One fortunate turn of events was that Striker now possessed a teleporter, which could accomplish his goal and was simple to use. In addition, the WLA was still well hidden in his basement and only a computer chip away from being operational.

Now his problem was to decide where and when to go back in time to produce a ripple point. He knew he had to act fast, as his current life as CEO of Mannaco was about to come to an end. It was just a matter of time before either the FBI or Gullon arrested him.

Striker went to his computer and spent the next two hours reviewing history and archeology for clues. It was now 11:00 A.M. and he made his decision. He would return to the United States in 1942 and sabotage the Manhattan Project!

It must have seemed odd for Otto to be ordered to purchase a 1940s suit and other articles of clothing from a specialty clothing store for his boss. Fortunately, Los Angeles is the city to be in for such a need. It is nice to be consistent in the city of inconsistencies.

By 2:00 P.M. Striker was ready and set the teleporter for 1942. He was instantly sent back in time. Michele had gone to her office several hours before and Bob was alone when he received the signal notifying him of Striker's destination.

Bob alerted Nova and she instantly teleported him the necessary clothes. He called Michele to let her know his plans and teleported to 1942 to stop and arrest Striker.

TTSA Bob Gullon arrived in Washington, D.C., in 1942 fully dressed as a local citizen, but not knowing where exactly Striker was or what he might be up to. Bob settled into his hotel to plan his next move. He purchased a local newspaper on this August afternoon and read a rather interesting article.

The United States had entered World War II by now and the article described how President Franklin Delano Roosevelt responded to the discovery of nuclear fission in 1939 by creating the Uranium Committee to investigate the possibility of making an atomic bomb. This project was just recently placed under U.S. Army control and named the Manhattan Engineer District (MED) under the direction of General Leslie Groves.

That was all Bob needed to know. This project was to be known as the Manhattan Project and its failure would create the ripple point Striker was planning. Bob immediately notified Nova from his portable hologram resonator and she sent him a complete description of the Manhattan Project.

When the United States spread its influence over the Philippines, Japan probably saw the United States as a threat in their imperialistic dreams in the Orient. Japan took advantage of World War II and began to pursue expansion in the Pacific. Japan responded to the American threat with a sneak attack when they bombed Pearl Harbor on December 7, 1941. The United States then entered World War II aligned with the Allied powers and ended up fighting Japan, predominantly on its own in the Pacific.

The first major challenge faced in the Manhattan Project was the ability to find an acceptable and plentiful source of fuel for the bombs. Neils Bohr stated that the isotope Uranium-325 (U-325) was a likely candidate because it was unstable and could sustain a chain reaction. Obtaining this element was a major challenge. The second major struggle in the project was being able to sustain a fission chain reaction, which gives the atomic bomb its power.

From the uranium ore, two types of isotopes are extracted; one is U-235 which makes up about one percent of the uranium ore, and the other is U-238 which makes up ninety-nine percent of the uranium ore. U-238 is useless in making an atomic bomb, but U-235 can be used in the bomb because it can sustain a chain reaction. U-235 is obtained from uranium ore, a natural rock containing the element. The uranium ore is then processed to extract the different uranium isotopes.

The task to separate the different uranium isotopes proved to be a major obstacle for the scientists. The first method that could be used to separate the isotopes was called magnetic separation. This process was made possible when Ernest O. Lawrence invented the cyclotron at the University of California, Berkeley, laboratories. After millions of dollars in construction, only about a gram of U-235 was produced.

Lawrence was upset that Robert Oppenheimer was appointed the weapons director of the project and that his laboratory, Los Alamos, would be used as the location of the weapons development instead of the Berkeley laboratory.

A second method of separation was used. In 1942 General Leslie Groves purchased a section of land in Oak Ridge, Tennessee, in order to construct a uranium separation facility. This facility used the principle of gaseous diffusion to separate the uranium isotopes. This process was an efficient and effective method for producing the required U-235.

The atomic bomb works on the principle of fission. Fission occurs when the central part of an atom, the nucleus, breaks up into two equal fragments. Once a neutron breaks up the uranium atom, the fragments release other neutrons that break up more atoms and so on. This chain reaction takes place in only millionths of a second. The amount of power released during this chain reaction is about several hundred million volts of energy, which are released at detonation. Neils Bohr paved the way towards the discovery of fission with his studies of atoms.

The only nuclear test explosion, code-named Trinity, was of a plutonium device; it took place on July 16, 1945, near Alamogordo, New Mexico. The first uranium bomb ("Little Boy") was delivered untested to the army and was dropped on Hiroshima on August 6, 1945, killing at least 70,000 inhabitants. On August 9, 1945, a plutonium bomb ("Fat Man") virtually identical to the Trinity device, was dropped on Nagasaki, killing at least 35,000 inhabitants.

Bob deduced that Striker would first go after

General Leslie P. Groves, the MED commanding officer. Striker posed as an army Pentagon officer and attempted to convince General Groves that he should focus on Ernest Lawrence's cyclotron at the University of California at Berkeley and the magnetic separation process.

General Groves planned to purchase land in Oak Ridge, Tennessee, to apply gaseous diffusion in order to separate the uranium isotopes. After much debate General Groves rejected Striker's analysis and left the building to go home. Striker followed him and planned to kill the general, but observed Bob Gullon tailing the general and left the road quickly. Bob tried to follow Striker, but traffic and skilled maneuvering by Striker prevented him from doing so.

Striker escaped and was foiled in the first phase of his plan. Bob knew that there would be no future attempts on general Groves's life by Striker. So what was Striker's next step?

Bob quickly deduced that the facility at Oak Ridge, Tennessee, would be Striker's next target. His teleporter could track Striker only when Striker leaped back or forward in time. Since Striker was a timeliner, Bob could not track him from location to location.

It was a gamble to go to Oak Ridge, but Bob chose to go anyway. During the next two days following Bob's arrival at Oak Ridge, he remained invisible through the use of his MCR and studied the facility. There were just too many ways Striker could destroy this plant.

Bob knew from Nova's research that when Enrico Fermi built a small reactor at the University of Chicago in 1942 under their squash courts, the controllable chain reactions produced still had possible dangers of instability. This precisely is why General Groves selected a location in Hanford, Washington, that was isolated and secure and relocated Fermi's lab there.

On the evening of the second night Bob observed a suspicious man in the facility. He was too far away to identify, so Bob moved closer. A security guard shared Bob's suspicion and approached this man. Suddenly, the suspicious man drew a phaser and killed the guard. Bob knew it had to be Striker, disguised by his own MCR.

Since Bob was not a timeliner, Striker's teleporter immediately alerted him to Bob's presence and Striker teleported out of the facility. Bob had won round two, but he knew that it was a matter of time before Striker scored a victory. It is far easier to alter events in history when you have 36th-century technology at your disposal than it is to prevent them.

Neils Bohr was a Jewish physicist from Denmark who escaped his homeland in 1943 when the Nazis occupied that country. He earned his doctorate in physics at the University of Copenhagen in 1911. Bohr was able to merge the Rutherford model of the atom with the new idea of quanta that had been put forth by Max Planck. This new model of the atom came to be known as the Bohr model, and won him the 1922 Nobel Prize in physics.

Bohr was to be a crucial member of the Los Alamos team with his background on splitting the atom. Striker's plan now was simple. All he felt he had to do was kill Bohr and this would delay the development of the atom bomb resulting in a ripple point. Striker teleported to 1943 and Bob was alerted to his destination.

Historically Striker knew that Bohr would take a fishing boat to Sweden and from there Bohr was flown to England to work on nuclear fission. A few months following that trip Bohr would join a British research team to Los Alamos to join Robert Oppenheimer's group and the Manhattan Project.

Striker felt his best shot at killing Bohr would be on the fishing boat. Now posing as a Danish fisherman, he approached Neils Bohr as the latter was about to board the fishing boat. Striker drew his phaser and was about to fire when Bob appeared and projected a red luminous ball at Striker just in time to prevent his assassination of Dr. Bohr. Striker demonstrated excellent reflex and teleported from the scene, knowing full well that Bob would have to remove the memories of this incident from Dr. Bohr and the fishermen present.

Bob was frustrated. Yes, he saved the life of Neils Bohr, but he let Striker escape again. This was becoming a pattern that Bob simply didn't want repeated.

Since Bob correctly deduced that Striker's mission was to sabotage the Manhattan Project, he guessed that Striker's next move would be at Los Alamos. He just didn't know when.

Michele was finding her attempts to gather evidence against Striker and Mannaco frustrating. It had been two days since Bob left and her contacts appeared to dry up one at a time. She knew Striker was a criminal in the 21st-century (to say nothing of the 36th-century). There was no way she could obtain a search warrant on

Mannaco or relate Bob's presence to Drake Collins.

She did report the warehouse incident to him, only because her gun was found there. She could have told him about the kidnapping, but there was no evidence that Striker himself was involved. All she could do was arrest Otto Schmidt. Bob instructed her not to do that yet, as he was a potential source in locating Striker, should the latter return to the year 2005.

Michele couldn't even find out where Striker lived. He had several properties around the world and in the greater Los Angeles area, but no one knew which one was his private residence. Striker was a private man who was known to purchase real estate through a series of dummy corporations and limited partnerships. This made it difficult, if not impossible, to locate these homes.

Because Striker was such a private man, he never hosted parties and always insulated himself from people who needed to communicate with him. He used cell phones, mail drops and other methods to maintain his privacy. Nobody at Mannaco knew where he lived.

Michele was concerned about Otto Schmidt. He had previously kidnapped her and already tried to kill her. She knew that Otto was more concerned with Bob, but that did not reduce her anxiety level. Criminals like Otto Schmidt did not fear the FBI or any other authority. They simply lived in their own world of ignoring rules and doing whatever they pleased.

Her warrant checks on Otto with the NCIC, FCIC, Warrant Information and Interpol turned out negative. Although he had files with several intelligence agencies, he was never arrested and no agency was hunting him down. This further added to Michele's frustration.

Just then her phone rang and her sixth sense told her that it was Assistant Director Drake Collins. She was right.

"Peterman, come to my office immediately," ordered Drake.

"Yes sir. I'll leave right now," she responded.

Michele entered Drake's office and was immediately admitted. It was 12:00 and she was starving. Drake Collins was standing by the large window adjacent to his desk. The noonday sun shone brilliantly around his silhouette. He remained frozen in this position as he spoke to Michele.

"What do you have to tell me about the warehouse incident?"

"Nothing more than what my report stated, sir," her words lacked conviction.

"It's not every day that one of my special agents loses her weapon at a crime scene. How do you expect me to handle the death of Alfred Doyle and the gangbanger?"

"I would leave that to the LAPD. If we get involved now with absolutely no evidence to tie in Striker, we could be left with egg on our face."

"Correction, Peterman. You would be left with egg on your face. Do I make myself clear?"

"Most definitely, sir."

"Get me something to justify a search warrant and let's get that son of a bitch. You are dismissed."

Michele could always tell when her boss was mad. His voice was always loud, but when he was truly angry he would resort to a military form of communication. Nobody else in her experience in the FBI would say, "You are dismissed."

Bob teleported to Los Alamos to prevent Striker's next move. His teleporter indicated that Striker arrived in 1945 and this was the most logical destination.

Another assassination attempt seemed unlikely. There was just too much security on the base. In June 1942 J. Robert Oppenheimer was appointed the technical director of the Manhattan Project. Under his guidance, the laboratories at Los Alamos were constructed. There he brought the best minds in physics to work on the problem of creating an atomic bomb. In the end he was managing more than three thousand people, as well as tackling theoretical and mechanical problems that arose. This is why Oppenheimer is referred to as the "father" of the atomic bomb.

Bob did a lot of thinking about where Striker might succeed in sabotaging the Manhattan Project at this late date. What was vulnerable? Both the uranium bomb destined for Hiroshima on August 6 and the plutonium bomb scheduled for Nagasaki had many safety features such as lead shields, fuses and neutron deflectors.

Because uranium is more fissionable, the bomb would be based on a gun-type detonator. Basically, a section of uranium would be shaped with a center section missing. The center section, a perfect fit, would be placed away from the large uranium mass. A conventional explosive would be used to propel the center section into the large section. Both sections would then weld together and start the reaction. The bomb would explode above the ground.

With the plutonium bomb the initial explosion would be made by a conventional explosive. This bomb was also designed to explode above the ground. Fuses were used as a guard against premature explosion of the nuclear elements and the conventional explosives. The fuses would be installed just minutes before the bombs were launched.

That was it! The fuses were among the vulnerable aspects of the bombs. Striker would know that and devise a plan to somehow compromise its function.

It was now early July and General Groves scheduled a test for July 16. The test site, named Trinity by Oppenheimer, was located in the valley between the Rio Grande river and the Sierra Oscura mountains. The locals referred to it as the Jordada del Muerto.

About 100 tons of TNT and some very valuable plutonium were used to calibrate measuring equipment and test radioactive fallout. At 4:00 A.M. the test began. The resulting explosion was equivalent to about 20,000 tons of TNT and over 100,000 photographs were taken to document this event.

The success of the test now led to the final stages of use for the atomic bomb. Striker became invisible and initiated several procedures to sabotage the fuses in both bombs. He was able to work undetected and Bob could only wonder where he was.

This was an uncomfortable twist that Bob feared. He knew Striker was not trained as a chrononaut and would not know about functioning in the fifth dimension remaining undetected by those living in the three-dimensional universe. Bob could not track Striker now and had to wait for him to reappear in order to deal with him.

It was now August 6 and the plane carrying the uranium bomb was on its way to Hiroshima. Due to a defective fuse the bomb would not detonate and it fell to the ground as a dud. There were other elements of Striker's sabotage that Bob could only consider after the fact.

The Nagasaki bombing was canceled and the Japanese surrender was delayed until 1946. Germany had already surrendered in May of 1945, so the fate of WWII was sealed. It required the deaths of several hundred thousand soldiers to finally capture Tokyo.

The United States did eventually construct a workable atomic and later hydrogen bomb, but not until the Soviet Union accomplished this feat. Bob knew this was a serious ripple point. He contacted Nova immediately.

"What does this mean to Striker's plan?" asked Bob.

"Well, hotshot, I have good and bad news. The good news is that there is no black hole as yet. The bad news is that our calculations reveal a ripple point of such proportion that one more such incident will generate the black hole in question."

"What do you want me to do now?"

"Bob, I suggest you return to 2005 and wait for Striker's next move."

Seven

Michele had made much progress during the past few days gathering evidence against Striker and Mannaco. She felt guilty about not informing Drake Collins about Otto Schmidt and his attempted murder and kidnapping of her. She didn't even tell him that she was staying in Woodland Hills!

Thanks to cell phones people are accessible no matter where they reside. How do you tell the assistant director of the Los Angeles Bureau of the FBI that you are temporarily residing in the residence of a time traveler from the 36th-century?

The FBI's contacts revealed four crime syndicate heads that have in the past, and are currently, doing business with Striker and Mannaco. They are all linked by rumor to have murdered the CEOs of the oil companies that exposed Mannaco's alternative fuel, and the senator and two congressmen who were found dead under somewhat suspicious circumstances.

There was no hard evidence to tie these murders, drug dealers and money laundering in with Striker yet. That was Michele's job. She reviewed the names of these crime bosses. There was Fabrizio Romano from Detroit, Vincenzo Bellani located in Chicago, Pasquale DeNardo working out of New York, and Lorenzo Giamona doing business in Miami.

All she had were rumors. Her next step was to pay a visit to each boss and see whet she could find out. She still didn't have the required probable cause for a search warrant. What she did know from her training and experience was that crime bosses knew everything about their business. Fabrizio Romano in Detroit was the first person she would visit.

Otto Schmidt has specific orders from Striker. The top priority was to rid themselves of Bob Gullon and Special Agent Michele Peterman. Next on his hit list were the four crime bosses that blackmailed Striker into doing business with them.

The various people that Striker needed killed were taken out by crime bosses Fabrizio Romano, Vincenzo Bellani, Pasquale DeNardo and Lorenzo Giamona. Striker ordered Otto to eliminate them at any cost before Striker teleported back to 1943. Otto did not know where his boss was going or for how long. All he knew was that he had a job to do. His job was murder.

Otto looked upon this assignment with pleasure. He considered this job at hand to be the closing of the pipeline. Striker's strategy was simple. If you eliminate the crime boss the others will cover their tracks, accept a new leader and make it easier for Striker to function without fear of reprisals.

The flight to Detroit was uneventful. Otto didn't plan to stay long. He overnighted his Walther PPK and Braush silencer to a special mail drop and retrieved it upon his arrival.

He knew exactly where Romano's headquarters was in downtown Detroit and made his way into the reception room, fingering his gun along the way. When Otto entered the room he quickly observed Romano's secretary. Her face and body were those of a very healthy and extremely attractive woman in her mid-forties, but somehow her pale blue eyes gave him a feeling that she was much older.

What immediately attracted Otto's attention was the midnight-blue sequined purse on her desk, as she was checking her makeup for the eighth time that day. Inside that eight-inch purse resided a pearl-handled German-made stainless steel knife and a slender five-inch blade. She knew whom she worked for.

Otto was unaware of her knife and it wouldn't have concerned him anyway. He quickly drew his gun and fired point blank at her chest. She was killed instantly.

With his gun still in his hand, Otto went to the office door and opened it. Fabrizio Romano was standing next to his desk changing a CD, unaware of the silent murder that Otto just committed. When he turned to face Otto, Romano stood as still as a statue.

It was as if Romano was in a deep hypnotic trance. Otto coldly fired three shots at Romano. One landed in his neck, one in the heart and the third in the stomach. Only the bullet in the heart was necessary to end the life of one of Detroit's crime bosses.

Michele was busy at her desk preparing for the trip to Detroit. A shot of ice-cold apprehension burst through her as she realized that she was not alone. Drake Collins was standing behind her.

"You can forget about going to Detroit, Peterman."

"What happened, sir?"

"Our friend Romano was found dead in his office an hour ago. He was shot by some unknown assailant."

Michele knew who killed Romano. Proving it was another matter. She now changed her plans and prepared to fly to Chicago ASAP.

But wait! Otto had obviously beaten her to the punch, so to speak. Why not use the teleporter and save the American taxpayers some airfare and obtain an advantage on a maniacal killer? Michele went to the Woodland Hills safehouse and reviewed the instructions Bob had given her regarding the teleporter and instantly relocated to the Windy City. During her teleportation Michele could hear her own voice and feel her body above her.

This was Michele's first trip to Chicago. She had read about this city in the past and was aware of its nickname the "Windy City" originating not from the gusty winds of Lake Michigan, but from Chicago's reputation as a city with boisterous politicians.

She was amazed at the sight of the cream-colored Wrigley Building on Michigan Avenue greeting visitors along the busy Michigan Avenue Bridge. The tallest bank building in he world, the First National Bank Building, also made this city unique.

In addition to its tall and imposing buildings, Michele was struck by Chicago's sculpture. Imposing pieces by such greats as Alexander Calder, Claes Oldenberg, Marc Chagall and Pablo Picasso distinguished the surrounding pedestrian plazas.

Vincenzo Bellani was known as an ardent Chicago Bear fan. He attended every Bear home game, unless a drug deal or other important criminal enterprise surfaced at the last minute on a Sunday afternoon. Michele knew what he looked like and where his box seat was located, and headed for Soldiers Field.

Otto Schmidt also knew that Vincenzo Bellani would be at the Bear game. Otto stayed in a luxury hotel suite that featured a roomy living room with a large bay window overlooking Lake Michigan. The thick pile of the carpet was beige, and the sofas and easy chairs were covered in white moiré silk. He checked his gun and silencer and headed for Soldiers Field to pay his deadly respects to one Vincenzo Bellani.

Michele arrived at Bellani's box seat first and flashed her FBI credentials as she introduced herself. Bellani quickly dismissed the young blond girl with the model figure and perfect features sitting to his right.

"Why don't you go powder your cute little nose and bring back some beer and hot dogs?" he told her.

"That's no way to treat one of your bimbos, Bellani," Michele commented as she watched the blond disappear into the runway.

"What do you want, Special Agent Pig?" Bellani

retorted defiantly.

"The FBI has quite a bit of evidence against you, but we are far more interested in your dealings with Mustafa Striker."

"What dealings?"

"You know, money-laundering."

"I admit nothing. You should be speaking to my mouthpiece, little girl."

Just then Otto reached for his gun. He was standing about twenty feet away and fired three shots directly at Bellani. Bellani moved to his left just in the nick of time to avoid the bullets which hit the back of his chair.

Michele turned in the direction of the shots and ordered Otto to freeze. He snaked through the now screaming group of people around him making his escape. Bellani disappeared and Michele headed for the parking lot.

As she approached it she saw Bellani take off in his Mercedes sports car. Michele spotted a Ford Bronco coming her way and flagged him down. She showed her FBI credentials, gave the driver her card and commandeered the vehicle in pursuit of Bellani.

Suddenly, there was the sound of screeching tires behind them. Michele saw a Jaguar racing up behind them as they traveled north on Lake Shore Drive. Otto fired a shot at Bellani and the bullet flattened Bellani's right rear tire. He turned off on Roosevelt Road and ran into the Field Museum across from Grant Park.

Michele cut off the cross traffic, nearly causing a pileup. Horns blared and brakes squealed as the other cars maneuvered out of the way. Otto got out of his Jaguar and ran after Bellani. Michele was on his tail and drew her gun.

Otto chased Bellani into one of the exhibit buildings and Michele lost them. Bellani ran up to the second floor and Otto fired a shot. Bellani was hit in the left arm and jumped out of the second story window to elude Otto.

Vincenzo landed on the asphalt, on his stomach. He looked up. He was dazed, cut and bleeding. He stared helplessly back over his shoulder at the building he just jumped out of and got up. Bellani found a spot in the back of a nearby building and dropped back against the wall to catch his breath.

Michele spotted Bellani and ran toward him. Bellani spotted a Honda parked near the building and ran toward it. Exhausted, he opened the door and looked for the key to the ignition. It's wasn't there, so he hot-wired the ignition and the car started.

Bellani put the car in gear, but froze as he felt a smooth, polished barrel of a gun against the back of his head.

"Turn the engine off and place both hands on the steering wheel now," demanded Otto.

Bellani did as he was told and as soon as the engine was turned off, Otto pulled the trigger and splat the windshield with Bellani's brain.

Suddenly, an advanced technology helicopter, seen only as an ominous black silhouette, hovered above the Honda. Its rotors were relatively quiet, not making the familiar loud THUD! THUD! THUD! of a normal chopper. The chopper descended to the ground and a familiar voice was heard.

"Get in, Otto," Striker commanded.

The helicopter rose quickly and moved fast in the direction of Michele. She ran into a statue of Lincoln and fell unconscious. The helicopter rose higher and was out of sight in less than a minute.

Michele regained consciousness a few hours later and had no idea who she was. Her run-in with the statue had caused amnesia. She walked around aimlessly for about thirty minutes when suddenly a vaguely familiar figure approached her. He had been observing her for five minutes. He removed an odd-looking pen flashlight from his pocket, shining it on Michele's eyes and forehead. She looked at him with recognition and started to cry.

"I am a complete failure. That is the second crime boss I let Otto kill. What am I going to do, Bob?"

"First let's get your FBI credentials and gun that you left by Lincoln's statue and then we'll go home. Do you still have your teleporter?"

"Yes. How did you know I teleported to Chicago?"

"We have our ways, my dear. My teleporter is automatically signaled when you use yours. It pinpoints exactly where you arrive and the biochip I implanted in your neck led me to you here in Grant Park."

They both teleported back to Woodland Hills and Bob briefed her as to his failure with the Manhattan Project.

"How serious is this?" she asked.

"It's a problem, but not that big a problem yet. Striker fully intends to make it a really big problem, unless I can stop him."

Bob explained to her the details of the ripple point created by the Manhattan Project mission failure and Nova's ability to measure the resulting ripple points. He asked her about her progress with gathering evidence against Mannaco and sympathized with her frustration.

"Michele, I can relate to minor failures in a mission. Always remember, it's the big picture that counts."

"Thanks for your support. It still doesn't make it easier for me. I must succeed with DeNardo and Giamona."

"What will you do now?" Michele queried.

"I am going to check in with Nova and wait for Striker's next move back in time. Any progress on finding out where he lives here in Los Angeles?"

"No. It's still a mystery. While you are checking in with your office, I will do the same with mine and see about the location of the other two crime bosses."

Michele called in to her office and was told that one of their informants stated that Pasquale DeNardo and Lorenzo Giamona were to soon meet in New York City. This was confirmed by a wiretap at one of DeNardo's restaurants.

Her office had plane tickets to New York ready for her, so teleportation was not going to be her mode of travel this time. She didn't want to tell them, "Oh, by the way, I won't need plane tickets because I can get to New York instantly with my 36th-century teleporter."

Eight

Drake Collins was not a happy man. He read Michele's report about the Chicago incident and was definitely not pleased. Not only was Vincenzo Bellani not interrogated, he was killed and the high-speed chase and dangers to the citizens of Chicago led to the Chicago bureau chief chewing out Drake. Assistant Director Collins did not like having to explain the actions of his special agents.

Michele also failed to protect Fabrizio Romano in Detroit and this further angered Drake. He summoned her into his office prior to her departure to New York.

"Peterman, do I have to stress the importance of your trip to New York?" Drake was impatient and angry.

"No sir, you don't. You have my two reports. Did you issue a warrant for Otto Schmidt yet?"

"Yes, that has been taken care of. We don't know

112

where he is and we have nothing on Striker."

"Is the warrant for Otto going to cause political problems regarding Striker?" she asked.

"Of course it is. It already has. Striker is well connected and the bureau wants us to get him real bad," Drake stated as he pounded his fist into his desk.

The two crime bosses, Pasquale DeNardo and Lorenzo Giamona, must not meet the same fate as has befallen Fabrizio Romano and Vincenzo Bellani. DeNardo and Giamona were her last leads to busting Striker and she knew she must not fail.

Michele tried to clear her mind of this stress and focused on Bob Gullon. She could not get this futuristic time traveler out of her mind. Yes she was attracted to him on several levels, but there seemed to be some unknown force preventing her from acting on her feelings. She wondered whether Bob felt the same way, but was afraid to ask him.

When Bob debriefed her following the Chicago trip and her first experience with teleportation, she had lots of questions. Michele read many books about the fifth dimension, but was still confused about its existence.

Bob explained that we can only observe three dimensions (length, width and depth) with our physical eyes. Time is considered the fourth dimension and any dimension beyond time is classified as the fifth dimension. The astral plane, where the soul travels upon death, is an example of the fifth dimension, as are parallel universes. Since our physical eyes cannot see time or the fifth dimension, most of mankind has been ignorant of their existence.

The identification with the physical body is considered scientific fact by Western science. As part of this illusion the public is brainwashed to think:

- There is no soul.
- Only physical life exists. There is no afterlife.
- Consciousness is a component of the physical brain and ceases to exist when the body dies.

It is only through awareness and knowledge that we can defeat this ignorance. Socrates said, "Knowledge is virtue." Each of these other dimensions (astral, causal, mental and etheric) have their own spiritual bodies.

To keep the conversation simple Bob focused on the astral plane with its respective astral body (double). He equated the classic out-of-body experiences (OBEs) with teleportation with one exception. In OBEs it is the astral body that travels. Teleportation involves the physical body itself moving from point A to point B. In both instances these bodies travel through the fifth dimension.

He pointed out the fact that all dreams are examples of OBEs and if you are conscious of leaving the physical body, it will result in a dream of rising into the air. Dreams of floating or flying often accompany being aware of moving horizontally, and falling dreams are the product of being conscious of returning to the physical body.

One classic example of an astral body appearing many miles away from the physical (known as bilocation) was documented by the Catholic Church in 1774. On September 17 of that year Alphonse de Liguori, imprisoned at Arezzo, remained quiet in his cell and took no nourishment. He was suffering from a variety of crippling diseases and entered into a cataleptic state, remaining motionless in his cell.

When he woke up five days later he announced that he had been at the bedside of the dying Pope Clement XIV and that the Pope was now dead. The startled monks dismissed this story as pure fantasy. Rome was at least four days away by horse and carriage, and there had been no official word of Clement's condition.

The news came a few days later that the Pope had died and that Liguori had been seen at the bedside of the dying Pope on the very day he died by the superiors of the Dominicans, Observatine, and Augustinian orders. The case was documented and accepted by the Catholic Church as a true bilocation.

Using the analogy of OBEs made it easier for Michele to comprehend the concept of teleportation. Bob went on to describe the mechanism of a typical OBE. The separation of the astral body from the physical commonly begins at the hands and feet and ends at the head. Blackouts and clicking or buzzing sounds at the moment of complete separation are frequently reported.

A feeling of paralysis is noted and then suddenly the individual sees himself floating in the air. Now one can observe his physical body beneath himself and the rest of the room, from a totally independent perspective. In an instant the individual returns to the physical body, often preceded by another momentary blackout.

During the OBE the subject may observe other doubles, which may appear as a close resemblance of the physical body, a glowing ball of light (most commonly blue, white or gold) or a pinpoint in space with circular vision.

The double's appearance may range from just a wispy presence to a very solid three-dimensional body that walks, talks, and breathes exactly as the physical body does. This double often appears larger, stronger, and much younger than its physical counterpart. Its movements are more agile and it seems to give off a light of its own. The double can see quite well without glasses, if such aids were required by the physical body.

The movement of the double varies from a zig-zag, or spiral movement, to a straight line path. Often streaks of light are seen behind the voyager. This astral light functions to assist in the doubles movement and allows the spiritual body to access their Akashic records (detailed accounts of past, present and future lives).

Often voyagers hear popping and buzzing sounds. In addition, a chorus of disembodied voices can be heard as if they were being whispered directly into the ear. A feeling of being bobbed about in a rowboat and often swaying sensations can now be felt.

In the fifth dimension you can see in a 360-degree circle through your astral eyes. This ability to view any environment from simultaneous and multiple points of view is called *omniscient* sight.

The double is often ovoid in form or is seen within an egg-shaped envelope. It gives off a glow that illuminates even a totally dark room. When in the fifth dimension voyagers feel no weight nor are they aware of heartbeat, breathing or other functions of their physical bodies.

Most commonly the double travels at the speed of light. The speed of travel may be so fast that the voyager may not be conscious most of the time of covering vast stretches of territory. They just think of where they are going and immediately find themselves there.

It is easy to become disoriented when in the fifth dimension. All you have to do is stare at a bright object to stabilize yourself. Time travel is most definitely possible while traveling in the fifth dimension. Since we enter the space-time continuum once we leave the physical body, there is no past or future. All time is simultaneous. These concepts are accepted by quantum physics, hyperspace physics and the Superstring theory of the 21st-century.

All throughout this conversation Bob could feel an immense attraction to Michele. She was not just a beautiful, intelligent and spiritual woman, there was something he couldn't define. At the same time he also felt that something was preventing him from acting on his feelings. Something other than the fact that it was a no-no with both agencies.

Pasquale DeNardo sat in his office on Fifth Avenue overlooking Central Park anticipating his lunch meeting with Lorenzo Giamona. The room was at least twenty-five feet square and seemed huge with just the three chairs and no other furniture. His large plasma TV was turned to CNN and he laughed as heard about the administration's prediction of a significant reduction in illegal drug trafficking.

What was funny about this news report was the alliance Pasquale had forged with Lorenzo regarding expanding their respective drug operations. These two crime bosses represented some of the largest importers and distributors of the major illegal recreational drugs brought into America.

Michele had time to take a nap on her flight from LAX to JFK airport in New York City. She vaguely recalled a dream fragment from her nap. The setting was in the future and she was some type of warrior dressed in a jumpsuit and using very advanced weapons in her role as protector of the universe.

She was looking forward to this trip. New York is a city of such extremes that any visitor would be hard-pressed to describe it without resorting to superlatives. Words like biggest and best come to mind when referring to America's most populated city. The enormous number of people, pace of life and stark urban landscape contribute to an often grim and sometimes frustrating experience when walking along its streets. More than eight million people live in the city's metropolitan area, which includes Long Island and parts of southern New York State, northeastern New Jersey and southwestern Connecticut.

Pasquale made reservations at the 21 Club for 1:00 P.M. This was his favorite restaurant in the city. Its location at 21 West 52nd Street next to Rockefeller Center was ideal. He loved the semiformal attire requirement and its colorful miniature statuary and black, wrought-iron fence surrounding the entrance.

DeNardo always liked to be ten minutes late for an appointment. It made him feel superior to have the other person wait for him. When he arrived at the 21 Club Lorenzo Giamona was patiently waiting and had ordered his usual scotch and soda.

The toys hanging from the ceiling of the restaurant only added to its whimsical decor. Pasquale ordered his favorite red wine after joining Lorenzo at the table.

"Excellent choice for our meeting, Pasquale," Lorenzo commented.

"It's good to see you again, my friend. We have much to discuss," DeNardo responded.

When the waiter returned to take their orders they both decided on the peppercorn-coated sirloin steak. Michele had arrived at the restaurant by 12:45 and was seated at the bar keeping an eye on both her prospects.

Just before she had the opportunity to approach both of them, a familiar and ominous figure dressed in a black suit, white shirt and black tie moved quickly to the table. He pulled out his Walther PPK with the Braush silencer and shot Lorenzo Giamona right between the eyes. Lorenzo slumped over onto the table and was dead instantly.

Pasquale acted quickly. He reached up and knocked the gun out of Otto Schmidt's hand and darted out of the restaurant. Michele was unable to get to either of them in the panic that ensued. When her path cleared they were both out of the restaurant and running toward

Fifth Avenue.

Michele had the foresight to retrieve Otto's gun and ran as fast as she could to catch up with them. Pasquale ran into St. Patrick's Cathedral to decide on his next move.

St. Patrick's Cathedral is a large building located on Fifth Avenue by 50th Street, not far from the 21 Club. It is one of the largest churches in America, with a seating capacity of 2,400. Its rose window is 26 feet across and the pipe organ has more than 7,380 pipes. Twin spires 330 feet high grace the 14th-century Gothic style structure.

The fact that Pasquale ran into the church did not appear to upset anyone. When Otto came in waving the spare gun he removed from his belt and lodged in the middle of his back, panic began. Several attendees in the church began to scream and Pasquale hid behind one of the benches.

Otto desperately searched the church looking for Pasquale. He was not going to let him escape again. The cashier at the souvenir stand located off the main entrance called the police on her cell phone as she darted out the building.

Michele was just a few hundred feet from the entrance of St. Patrick's Cathedral when she observed several dozen people running out screaming. She quickly surmised that this must be where Pasquale and Otto had run. She ran as fast as she could to the church with her gun in her right hand.

Inside the church things did not look good for Pasquale. He knew the police would arrive soon, but would they be in time to save him?

Otto narrowed his search to the benches that were located just below the rose window. He dropped to his knees to look for Pasquale's feet. Finally, he located Pasquale and called out to him.

"I got you, you bastard. Stand up and take it like a man," Otto demanded.

"Fuck you, kraut! Come and get me," snarled Pasquale.

With that remark Otto still on the ground, angled toward Pasquale and fired his spare Walther PPK without the Braush silencer.

BAM. BAM. BAM.

Because of the angle of the shot, the 26-foot rose window was hit and exploded above Pasquale's head. He lunged to avoid the falling glass and Otto fired two more shots that found their mark. One shot landed in Pasquale's stomach and the other in his heart. Otto quickly checked the body, saw Pasquale was dead and ran out of the church.

Five minutes later Michele arrived inside the church and saw Pasquale lying dead on the floor. The NYPD then arrived with their sirens blaring and she realized she failed again. The last two crime bosses were dead and she would have a lot of explaining to do. Dealing with the NYPD wasn't a big problem. It was Drake Collins Michele was concerned about.

Her flight back to Los Angeles was as depressing as attending a funeral. She called Bob on her cell phone and let him know that she would arrive shortly in Woodland Hills. Within ten minutes of her arrival Bob had some interesting news.

Michele briefed him on her New York trip and told him that Otto escaped again. He patiently listened to her and then informed her that Striker had teleported to New York. It was not to 2005, but 1780. He shocked Michele when he said, "You are coming with me."

Nine

"What do you mean I'm coming with you to 1780?" Michele asked.

"Look, I think you would be a great help in the mission. 'Two heads are better than one' is what people from your time used to say," Bob remarked.

"Isn't it against your agency's policies to recruit a non time traveler for a mission?"

"I admit that I haven't cleared this with Nova, but us chrononauts are given great latitude during a mission. If I decide in my best judgment that you would be an asset, then it is permissible. Besides, you are the only 21st-century citizen I can trust."

"Well, you don't have to convince me. I surely don't want to face Drake Collins now after I botched the New York assignment," Michele grimaced.

"You did your best in New York. How did you

know that a matter of a few minutes would make the difference in the killings of DeNardo and Giamona?" Bob exclaimed.

"But do you want an FBI agent who is zero for four in protecting targets?"

"I'm not worried about that. Remember, we have my experience and we outnumber Striker two to one."

Before they teleported to 1780, Bob gave Michele a complete briefing. The teleporter indicated that Striker's destination was Rockland County, New York. That meant absolutely nothing to Michele.

The West Point Military Academy is located in Rockland County, New York. Bob explained to Michele that Benedict Arnold was placed in charge of West Point and in 1780 attempted to turn this fort over to the British, which would cause the colonists to lose the American Revolutionary War of 1775-1783.

Michele knew very little about Benedict Arnold, so Bob gave her a thorough briefing. Benedict Arnold was born in Norwich, Connecticut, on January 14, 1741. Throughout his life Arnold was noted for his physical strength and bravery. He was a true romantic and excessively proud, sensitive and adventurous.

Arnold was also known to be governed more by impulse than by principle and this was to be his downfall in 1780. For example, at the age of fifteen he ran away from home and enlisted in the Connecticut army and marched to Albany and Lake George to assist the French invasion during the French and Indian War. However, becoming tired of that lifestyle he deserted and went home to Connecticut.

In Norwich he worked in a drug shop and later moved to New Haven. Here he opened a drug shop and became a bookseller. It was at this time that the ambitious Benedict Arnold acquired considerable property and engaged in the West India trade. Occasionally he would command his own ships.

After the Battle of Lexington in April 1775, Arnold raised an army of soldiers and offered to lead them to Boston. General Webster decided to wait for orders and refused to supply ammunition to Arnold's unit. When Arnold threatened to break into the munitions storage place, he was given the ammunition and his company marched to Cambridge, Massachusetts. This pattern of being turned down by authority figures and rebelling against their decision was to become a pattern throughout Arnold's career.

Arnold immediately proposed the capture of Ticonderoga and Crown Point, and the plan was approved by Dr. Warren, chairman of the Committee of Safety. Arnold was commissioned as colonel by the provincial Congress of Massachusetts, and directed to gather 400 men in the western counties and surprise the forts. The same scheme had been entertained in Connecticut, and troops from that colony and from Vermont (not yet a colony) through their leader Ethan Allen and his "Green Mountain Boys."

When Arnold's troops met with Ethan Allen's unit, Arnold claimed the command, but when it was refused he joined the expedition as a volunteer and entered Ticonderoga side-by-side with Allen. A few days later Arnold captured St. John's. Massachusetts asked

Connecticut to put him in command of these posts, but Connecticut preferred Allen.

After his success in the Ticonderoga campaign, Arnold proposed an expedition against Quebec to General George Washington. Arnold was placed in command of 1,100 men on this rather difficult and dangerous mission. He conducted this mission with great skill, but was nearly sabotaged by the misconduct of Colonel Enos, who deserted and returned to Massachusetts with 200 men and the greater part of the provisions. Arnold's force was insufficient to storm the city.

He received a wound in the leg. For his gallantry he was now made brigadiergeneral. He kept up the siege of Quebec until the following April. The British, being now heavily reinforced, were able to drive the Americans from Canada.

Problems haunted Arnold in the form of one Lt. John Brown of Pittsfield. Brown brought charges against Arnold of malfeasance while in the command at Montreal, with reference to exactions of private property for the use of the army. Arnold was exonerated and the report was confirmed by Congress. Nevertheless, a party hostile to Arnold had begun to grow up in that body.

On February 19, 1777, Congress appointed five new major generals: Stirling, Mifflin, St. Clair, Stephen, and Lincoln—thus passing over Arnold, who was the senior brigadier. None of these officers had rendered services at all comparable to his, and these appointments were made soon after his heroic conduct on Lake Champlain. This incident greatly angered Arnold, even though he agreed to serve under these less qualified generals.

In April 1977 the British troops under Governor Tryon invaded Connecticut. Arnold was on the scene with several hundred militia and drove the British to their ships. The British narrowly escaped capture by Arnold's troops. Even though Arnold was promoted to the rank of major general, his relative rank of seniority was not restored.

Later Washington convinced Arnold to join the northern army and the latter's brilliant strategy dispersed the British army of St. Leger, which, in cooperation with Burgoyne, was coming down the Mohawk valley, and had laid siege to Fort Stanwix. In the battle of September 19 at Freeman's farm, he frustrated Burgoyne's attempt to turn the Americans left, and held the enemy at bay until nightfall. If properly reinforced by Gates, he would probably have inflicted a crushing defeat upon Burgoyne. But Gates, who had already begun to dislike him, was enraged by his criticisms of the battle at Freeman's farm, and sought to wreak Arnold's effect by withdrawing from his division some of its best troops.

At the critical moment of the decisive battle of October 7 Arnold rushed upon the field without orders, and in a series of magnificent charges broke through the British lines and put them to flight. The credit of this great victory, which secured for us the alliance with France, is due chiefly to Arnold. At the close of the battle Arnold was severely wounded in the leg that had been hurt at Quebec. On January 20, 1778, Arnold received from Congress an antedated commission restoring him to his original seniority in the army.

On June 19 of that year, Washington placed Arnold in command of Philadelphia, since Arnold was too lame for field command. The British had recently evacuated from the city, and Tory (British) sentiment was quite strong. Arnold there met Margaret Shippen, a Tory sympathizer, and they were married.

It is during the next two years that Arnold socialized often with the Tories. He lived quite extravagantly and became heavily in debt. His new plan consisted of resigning his commission, obtaining a land grant in central New York and live the rest of his life in rural seclusion. His request was viewed favorably by the New York legislature, but a long list of charges now brought against him again forced him to abandon this plan.

The charges were investigated by a committee of Congress, and he was acquitted. Arnold then, considering himself vindicated, resigned his command of Philadelphia. But now a court-martial rendered its verdict on January 26, 1780, and agreed in every particular with that of the committee of Congress. It was decided that he should receive a reprimand from the commander-in-chief, Washington, who considered Arnold the victim of persecution, and couched the reprimand in such terms as to convert it into a eulogy. Washington soon afterward offered Arnold the highest command under himself in the northern army for the next campaign.

Arnold was given the command of the fort at West Point in July 1780 after he aggressively presented his case to General Washington. It was here that Benedict Arnold became a traitor.

The factors behind his decision were many. He fought brilliantly for the American cause for six years. He was badly wounded twice. Drawing deeply into his own purse to pay expenses, he was never reimbursed for most of them, nor honored by Congress for his victories. Three years had elapsed since Saratoga, and the fortunes of the Americans, instead of improving, had grown worse and worse. France had as yet done but little for the American cause. The colonial southern army had been annihilated. The paper money had become worthless, and credit abroad had hardly begun to exist.

Arnold now became frustrated, angry and depressed. He was approached by a Major John André of the British army, who convinced Arnold to turn over the West Point fort to the British. Arnold theorized that by putting the British in possession of the Hudson River, he would give them all they had sought to obtain by the campaigns of 1776-77. The American cause would become so hopeless that an opportunity would be offered for negotiation.

Arnold's plot was detected by the timely capture of André, who hid their plans in his boot. Three American soldiers found these plans and André was brought to George Washington's headquarters at Tappan in Rockland County on the west bank of the Hudson River near West Point. André was tried and executed as a spy. Arnold fled to the British army and was made a brigadiergeneral and paid a paltry sum of money.

Now Arnold fought for the British against the

Americans and was destined to go down in history as one of the most despised traitors known to mankind.

Michele absorbed this discussion and focused on the big picture. Bob was obviously concerned that Striker's plan was to somehow have Benedict Arnold succeed in his treachery and create a major ripple point.

"I can see now what Striker's plan is, Bob, but something about his Mannaco dealings still bother me."

"What's that?" Bob offered.

"If he became involved in money-laundering with the four now departed crime bosses because he needed his enemies eliminated, why not simply use Otto Schmidt to commit these murders?"

"My own research revealed that Striker did not meet Otto until 2002. The murders of the three oil company CEOs, two congressmen and one senator took place from 1999 to 2000."

"That explains it. The U.S. Attorney's office has sworn out a warrant for Otto's arrest, so I don't think he will be hanging around Mannaco's lab," replied Michele.

"I just received our clothing and additional research to assist us in our excursion to 1780. Do you have any questions before we leave?"

"Yes. Didn't it raise some eyebrows when you requested an 18th-century woman's outfit for this trip?"

"No, because the request goes directly to a robot. All chrononaut requests are automatically processed by machines. As I said before, we have much latitude on missions and our equipment requests are rarely questioned."

"What is our cover, Bob?"

"We will be traveling as husband and wife. My papers will identify me as Charles Madison from New York City and you are my wife, Katherine. I am a bookseller and we are on vacation."

"I guess that cover is necessary to explain me. Even I know that women didn't travel alone in 1780, least of all during a war."

"You are correct. Now let's review using the teleporter and the phaser. I don't' want 21st-century bullets found in 1780 should you have to fire a weapon. The phaser leaves no evidence. It kills the person internally."

Bob spent the next hour reviewing technical data and techniques and then both of them teleported to Rockland County, New York, in July 1780.

Upon their arrival in Rockland County Bob used some of the money he received from his department to purchase two horses and some supplies for the trip.

"We must blend in during our stay here, Michele. Teleporting around will raise too much suspicion and only foster the already high level of paranoia that exists here," Bob explained.

"I understand, Bob. After all, there is a war going on and we are strangers here."

They made their way to a local tavern to check for leads on Striker's whereabouts. A heated discussion was in progress between two of the locals, Andrew and John.

"What do you mean we can't win the war, Andrew? It's Tories like you that make me want to get my gun out and blow a few heads off, including yours."

"Look, John, we have known each other all of our

lives. I accept the fact that you are a radical and want the colonists to free themselves from England. It simply can't happen."

"Why not?" John asked.

"Your troops lack discipline. You have few weapons and sparse ammunition. Most of your soldiers are impatient farmers who return to their farms when they get bored."

"That may be so, Andrew, but our fighters are spread out over a large area with an endless wilderness behind it. We are experts on guerrilla tactics and have proven our ability to fight well in the open and destroy troops in movement."

"My dear friend John, the British have a well-drilled army, command of the sea and no other wars to distract them from their quest to put down this rebellion."

"You see, Andrew, we have no vulnerable capital and the best general imaginable in George Washington. The British generals are idiots. Remember what happened in Burgoyne in 1777 when he surrendered to our boys."

"That was a fluke," retorted Andrew.

"The hell it was. Following Saratoga both France and Spain sided with us and the French fleet has minimized the British advantage at sea."

"Britain still rules the water, John."

"Not only is England being drained financially, they are more concerned with protecting their Caribbean Islands like Jamaica from French takeover. Jamaica and other islands are far more valuable to England than us," replied John.

"What about the Hessian soldiers England has here?" Andrew asked.

"Those hired German troops have created far more problems with the British regulars than they have for us. Look what happened in Trenton in 1776."

"Yes, John, I am well aware of Washington's victory in Trenton on Christmas day of 1776, but he has lost almost all of the battles so far."

"All I say to you my friend is Tom Paine's *Common Sense* said it best: 'The blood of the slain, the weeping, voice of nature cries, Tis time to part.'"

Bob and Michele listened to this debate with great interest. It is important to get a feel for the locals in a time period. They both observed how Americans were divided about the Revolution. One third were loyal to England and were called Tories. Another third were neutral and the last third were for complete separation and were known as radicals.

Bob now approached the bartender to inquire as to the presence of Striker. Michele stared at the table and kept her eyes open for any trouble.

"Excuse me, bartender, but have you seen any strangers lately?" Bob asked.

"You and that woman are the only strangers I've seen today. What's your business in these parts anyway?" the bartender asked as he kept wiping off the counter as if it were some religious rite.

"My name is Charles Madison and that young lady is my wife, Katherine. We are on vacation visiting some of her relatives. I am looking for a heavy-set man about forty with a mustache. Have you seen such a person?"

"Now that you mention it, I have. A man fitting that description came around a few days ago asking about the fort at West Point. He seemed like an odd sort," responded the bartender.

"That's him. Do you know if he's staying in town?"

"Yep. He is at our only hotel up the street. Now if you'll excuse me I have to fill some orders."

Bob and Michele left the tavern and walked to the local hotel. They found out that Striker was staying there. The hotel clerk gave them suspicious looks and wanted to know why Bob was asking all those questions.

Suddenly, the clerk was called to leave the hotel by a boy carrying a message. The clerk's wife took over his position behind the counter.

"I know the man you're looking for. He talks a lot about the war. That is all people talk about. When we hear news of a battle, it is argued about at the tavern, and people take sides. You know, some people want England to win; others want us to be free."

"Yes, I'm sure. Do you know when to expect him back here?"

"No. You know this war has caused a lot of problems for this town. There are all kinds of fights, and sometimes people get killed just for expressing an opinion."

"That's the problem with wars. Have you seen any other strangers lately?" Bob asked.

"Well, now that you mention it, yes. There's this man John André and a woman traveling with him. I think her name is Beverly Robinson. He said she was his cousin."

"Do you know where they are now?"

"No, but they'll be back soon. Their clothes are still in their room. I just cleaned the rooms an hour ago."

Bob briefed Michele and they both decided to walk around town checking leads for André and Robinson. He told her that Beverly Robinson was an American Tory who was deeply involved in the treason plot with André against Benedict Arnold.

They went to the local stables and asked the man grooming a horse about Striker, André and Robinson. He didn't know anything about Striker, but did seem to know André and Robinson.

"Yes sir, I arranged for them to get some horses. She is an odd woman though."

"What is odd about her?" asked Bob.

"Well, she asked me what I thought about the war."

"What is unusual about that?"

"A lady just doesn't talk politics with a man."

"What did you tell her?"

"Oh, just the usual. I told her that I wasn't particularly interested in politics. She did ask me a lot of questions."

"Did she tell you her opinions of the war?"

"You know, it's funny. She asked me all those questions, but she never told me what her views were. I have no idea what she thinks about the war, no idea at all."

In a cabin just outside of town, British Major John André is meeting with Beverly Robinson. They are having tea and discussing their plan.

"I want to thank you for arranging the meetings with General Arnold, Beverly. You are doing a great service for your country," André stated.

"You don't have to convince me of my patriotic duty, Major André. My family does a lot of business with England and we have vested interests in putting down the American revolt."

"The fact that one of their best generals is on our side will only make our job easier," bragged André.

"Are you sure he is with us, Major?"

"Yes, most definitely. We have promised him a rank of brigadiergeneral and a stipend in cash."

André knew the amount of money Arnold was to receive was a paltry sum. The rank of brigadier-general meant nothing to the British army. He knew that England wanted to put an end to this financial drain and concentrate on the Caribbean and the war with France and Spain.

Beverly did not realize how ruthless André was. He thought nothing of keeping her on a string and using her for her family's contacts. It meant absolutely nothing to him that he was endangering her life, as well as that of her family. This is war and as a major in the British army André was used to risking his life. He had to succeed.

"You know I have always liked the crown. They founded the country, built the towns and roads and helped make us what we are today," she commented.

"Exactly. Just who is this George Washington anyway? Remember, he fought with us during the

French and Indian war and helped us rid the French from these colonies," André explained.

"I couldn't agree with you more, Major. Do you have the specific plans for General Arnold?"

"Yes. I will fold them up and place them in my boot. In a few days I am expected by General Arnold at West Point. I have to be careful, since it's located not far from General Washington's headquarters and security will be tight."

At Tappan in George Washington's New York headquarters a captain is briefing men and alerting them to reports of a British plot to take over the fort at West Point. They do not know who specifically is involved, but their orders are to make more patrols surrounding the trails going to West Point.

The soldiers were ordered to arrest anyone acting suspicious and to bring them back to the Tappan base. Shoot to kill orders were given to anyone fleeing or interfering in any way with their duties.

Back at the local hotel, Bob and Michele spoke to a seamstress who informed them of the house at the edge of town being used by Beverly Robinson and Major André. She informed them that both of them were seen meeting there. It was odd because they both had rooms in the hotel. Bob confirmed this with the hotel clerk's wife and he and Michele rode out to that cabin.

"Wouldn't it be faster to teleport out there?"

"Michele, we've gone through this before. It's imperative that we don't bring attention to ourselves. Sure we could teleport there, but how would we explain our quick arrival to someone passing by? With no horses they would probably burn us at the stake for practicing black magic."

"Bob, aren't you being a bit melodramatic?"

"Maybe so, but these are difficult times. Anything we do here can create ripple points."

"I am aware of that. If Striker is successful in helping Arnold, there'll be one hellava ripple point. Right?"

"I don't even want to think of the consequences. We must stop Striker ourselves."

"What do you mean, Bob?"

"Well, we can't very well go to Tappan and tell the army that we know who is going to commit treason because we are from the future and it made all of the history books!"

"Yes I get it."

"Remember, Benedict Arnold is today in 1780 considered a military hero and personal friend of George Washington. We have to act without their assistance," added Bob.

Bob and Michele mounted their horses and rode out to the cabin. They found the place empty. Bob utilized a special tracing device and was informed that Beverly and André had left just two hours before. His device cannot tell them where these two went. They rode back to the hotel somewhat frustrated and planned their next move.

Meanwhile at George Washington's New York headquarters at Tappan the soldiers were given another briefing. The army's intelligence had informed them that there is a British spy in the area. They do not know anything about his plans, but they do know he is working with an American Tory named Beverly Robinson.

An arrest warrant had been issued for her and the soldiers were instructed to be especially vigilant about strangers in the area. Beverly Robinson had been spotted traveling with a stranger within their vicinity.

What these soldiers could not have known was that during these briefings an unwanted visitor was eavesdropping in the fifth dimension. Striker had heard everything and planned to follow the patrols to assist Major André in his mission.

Striker overheard another piece of news which elated him. It seems that General Washington himself decided to make a surprise call on Benedict Arnold at the fort. This gave Striker the golden opportunity of assassinating Washington at the same time assisting the British army in taking over the fort and bringing the American Revolution to a quick and decisive end.

Bob and Michele now planned to explore the region in the fifth dimension and spend most of their time by Arnold's fort. There they hoped to intersect Striker and prevent his actions.

Major André went to see Arnold by a circuitous route. He knew that the well-traveled paths would be heavily patrolled and his best chances of getting through lay in an obscure path.

The trip was slow and tedious. Beverly Robinson had decided to wait for him at the hotel and return home after André completed his mission. Little did she know that the mission was about to benefit from a 36th-century man now also wanted for treason, murder and theft.

André arrived near the fort with his plans concealed in his boot. Suddenly, André heard the sound of horses coming. He could now make out three American soldiers ordering him to dismount immediately.

It would be foolish to attempt to kill these enemy soldiers. The best André could accomplish was to kill one of them before he himself was shot. André dismounted as the soldiers arrived.

They questioned him and were suspicious of André's demeanor and inability to explain his presence. One of the soldiers conducted a thorough search of André and found nothing incriminating.

Finally, one of the other soldiers ordered André to take off his boots. André protested, but was unable to prevent two of the soldiers from taking off his boots. When they discovered the plans folded up in one boot, the soldiers immediately placed André under arrest.

Just as this took place Striker made his appearance. He had observed this entire sequence and now held his phaser in hand and fired quickly, killing all three soldiers before any of them could detect him and fire first.

Striker then instructed André to continue on his trip, meet with Arnold and carry on his mission. André had many questions but Striker refused to answer them and returned to the fifth dimension.

André did meet with Arnold and the plans proved successful. Striker teleported the soldiers' bodies into the Hudson River. He weighted their bodies down so they would sink and remain deep under water.

When Bob and Michele arrived in the area later

they observed nothing unusual. After several hours of their patrol they teleported back to the hotel. During the next week nothing seemed out of order. Little did Bob and Michele know that the British had begun to execute André's plans.

Back at Tappan General Washington arrived and received a briefing prior to his short trip to see Benedict Arnold. He headed out on horseback and several miles later Striker appeared again. Washington didn't have a chance. The phaser instantly killed him and news about his assassination rocked Tappan and shocked the headquarters.

Bob and Michele naturally heard the disheartening news and realized they failed in their mission to stop Striker. There was nothing they could do now. They were informed of Washington's death about three hours after the fact.

"Isn't there anything you can do, Bob?"

"Unfortunately, no. My quantum medicine techniques can revive people who have been killed, but I must reach them within an hour of their death. Too much time has elapsed now."

They both teleported back to Woodland Hills in 2005, each dreading communication from their superiors. Meanwhile, the British army succeeded in taking Arnold's fort.

The news of Washington's death spread quickly. It demoralized the entire army and convinced France and Spain to terminate their support to the American cause. By the end of 1780 the colonial army surrendered and the American Revolution ended.

The first thing the British army did after securing the colonies was to issue arrest warrants for dozens of American patriots. Benjamin Franklin, Patrick Henry, Thomas Jefferson, John Adams, Samuel Adams, Alexander Hamilton, James Madison, John Hancock and the remaining signers of the Declaration of Independence were eventually caught, tried as traitors and hung.

Instead of a new free democratic country, free of monarchs, dukes, princes, counts, etc., the colonies still belonged to England. The four million Americans now had their fate determined by Benedict Arnold. It was Arnold alone who conducted the surrender negotiations.

In order to prevent further uprisings, the British government under Lord North agreed to the liberal terms previously offered them in 1778. The British conceded everything that the Americans had demanded in 1775.

Arnold was now looked upon as a hero by both the Americans and British alike. Instead of being labeled as a traitor, he was given the rank of brigadiergeneral and placed in charge of the entire British army in America.

This most disastrous result had far-reaching effects abroad. There was no French Revolution, no Napoleonic rule, no real threat to European monarchs. Even though America was eventually granted independence by 1850 and a Republican form of government established, the resulting political consequences created a huge ripple point.

In 3567 Nova received word of unusual disturbances around the planet. High winds appeared blasting through the girders of buildings. Bridges began to torque and appeared to be coming apart any minute.

The upper floors of several high-rise buildings exploded, showering the street with shattered glass. In the desert regions, the hurricane-free winds blasted the sand. Bodies lay dead on the ground, being quickly buried by the blowing sands. An ominous swirling vortex for the first time appeared in the sky, dimming out the sun. That was the beginning of the Apocalypse!

Ten

The next morning Michele awakened reluctantly reaching back into her dream state for some way to correct the mistakes of the trip back to 1780. This was far worse than being unable to prevent the killing of four crime bosses, or even gathering incriminating evidence. The resulting ripple point created could have disastrous consequences on the planet and the universe.

Bob also awoke stressed. He is used to a quality night's rest, but this did not happen. He awakened to a hologram signal from Nova. During the next hour Bob briefed Nova as to the events that transpired during the trip back to 1780.

"So, hotshot, you couldn't stop Striker in New York. We have big problems here."

"How big, Nova?"

"Well, a black hole has been sighted several

million miles from the Earth. It is moving toward us and beginning to create havoc. More disasters are being reported by the hour. Scientists are predicting the end of the world, as the Earth will eventually be sucked into it."

"Are you going to send additional help back?"

"No, our calculations tell us that would only worsen events and lead to more ripple points.

"I know you brought Special Agent Peterman with you. We have no problem with that, but expect no other chrononauts to assist you."

"Can you assist me locating Striker now? I must stop him before he creates more ripple points."

"You know I can't. That maniac is still a timeliner and it is only when he teleports back in time that you will be alerted as to his location."

"I really messed up by leaving him with a teleporter, didn't I? Without that he couldn't do any damage. His WLA doesn't work because of a faulty computer chip," Bob commented.

"Don't be too hard on yourself, Bob. We all make mistakes. Just stop him when he makes his next move."

"Just how bad is this black hole now, Nova?"

"Our people are panicking. There are examples of panic and chaos in the street. Terror has gripped many people and our police are experiencing great difficulty in trying to maintain order."

"What do your calculations show as to the precise effect of the two ripple points?"

"Well, Bob, it isn't good news. If Striker creates one more huge ripple point, he will succeed in his goal of destroying our galaxy. To do this he will have to travel much farther back in time and deal with even more significant historical events."

"Do you still want me to keep a computer chip record of these transmissions?"

"Yes. We want this documented for his trial and for our own use."

"You mean the training of future chrononauts?"

"Yes, exactly. That is assuming we are still around."

"You mean if my negligence doesn't lead to the destruction of our galaxy."

"Now now, Bob, you can't always be perfect. You couldn't possibly control events when you are fighting for your life and protecting Michele. It is most unfortunate that you left your teleporter with him. We don't blame you for that."

"That is nice of you to say, but it still doesn't make me feel better. I screwed up, as they say in 2005. Screwed up bad!"

"Keep your wits about you Bob and brief Peterman on anything she doesn't know that is necessary for her to assist you in the mission."

As Bob signed off he became lost in deep thought as to how to salvage this mission. He most definitely had a lot on his mind.

In his Calabasas estate Striker received a welcome communication from Drax.

YOU HAVE DONE WELL STRIKER. I ALMOST GAVE UP ON YOU AND YOU KNOW WHAT THAT WOULD MEAN. MY CALCULATIONS SHOW THAT WE NEED ONE

MORE SIGNIFICANT RIPPLE POINT. THIS MUST
TAKE PLACE AT LEAST 3,000 YEARS BACK IN
TIME FROM WHERE YOU ARE NOW. GO TO IT.

Striker left his special office in the basement of
this large multilevel home and returned to the main floor
to speak with his special guest.

"Otto, you are to stay here for a while. My sources
tell me the feds have issued a warrant for your arrest."

"But boss, what can I do?"

"First, keep away from the lab and our warehouses.
Just lay low. I will use my many political contacts to
handle this matter and strike the warrant," Striker lied.

"Right now all I want to do is kill that Peterman
bitch and that asshole Bob Gullon."

"No more killings, Otto. You have the feds after
you, along with four different crime families.
Fortunately none of them know about this home."

"So I am safe here?"

"Yes, as long as you stay put. Got it?"

"Yeah, I guess so," Otto responded. His face
blanked for a moment, then took on an expression of
milder concern.

Striker scrawled a note on a pad to himself and
placed it in his coat inner pocket and returned to his
basement office. Neither Otto nor anyone else knew of
this special underground floor to his estate. It is here
Striker kept the WLA. Even though it was nonfunctional
and currently useless to his plan, he liked to look at it.

Drake Collins reviewed a series of reports on his
desk dealing with Michele's progress and was visibly
angry. He pounded his right fist onto the top of his desk

for the third time before he summoned Michele into his office.

"Special Agent Peterman, give me one good reason why I shouldn't fire you, grind you up and feed you to the pigeons in the park!"

"Assistant Director Collins, I have tried my best and accept full responsibility for my actions. You have my reports, sir."

"I have sketchy reports with holes in them large enough to drive a truck through. I have no travel expenses from your Chicago trip, for example. Did you hitchhike there?"

"I used my own funds for that trip. Am I in deep trouble, sir?"

"Look, Peterman, we both know your record is excellent. I'm just troubled by this case. The events in Detroit, Chicago and New York read like a James Bond novel, to say nothing of the political ramifications," Drake appeared to calm down as he spoke.

"Political ramifications, sir?"

"Yes, Michele, you see now that we've issued a warrant for Schmidt's arrest, Striker's political contacts have been working overtime to keep us away from Striker and Mannaco."

Michele knew Drake was calm when he referred to her by her first name.

"You mean Striker is trying to quash Otto's warrant?"

"No. He doesn't give a damn about Schmidt. The only ass Striker wants to protect is his own."

"So what type of pressure are we getting, sir?"

"Congress mostly. Striker has many legislators on his side. Mannaco's recent cancer cure drug has established him and his company as the ultimate golden boy."

"You're saying we'd better be sure about our suspicions."

"Damn right! I know you have your suspicions that somehow didn't end up in your report, Michele. The bottom line is you've given me no hard evidence for us to act on Striker or Mannaco."

Michele almost started to describe Striker's attempt on her life at his warehouse, but thought better of it. How could she go into all the details without bringing Bob into it? She had to bide her time and assist Bob in his mission to prevent Striker from creating another ripple point. Everything about this case just paled in comparison to the big picture.

She left Drake's office with a sense of relief that she wasn't suspended or fired, but still frustrated and stressed. After more research and routine duties she left for Woodland Hills.

What Michele didn't know, as she traveled the 405 on her way to the San Fernando Valley, was that certain people were planning to deal with Otto Schmidt and Striker. In Detroit, Chicago, New York and Miami, the crime organizations of the late Fabrizio Romano, Vincenzo Bellani, Pasquale DeNardo and Lorenzo Giamona, respectively, were receiving their own intelligence reports.

The information these crime families obtained revealed that Otto Schmidt killed their respective bosses acting under the orders of Striker. Contracts were issued for both of their deaths. Their chief obstacle was in not knowing where Striker lived and where Otto was hiding out. They most certainly were going to look for them with orders of shoot to kill.

Bob continued his briefing of Michele on the teleporter, phaser and other weapons and procedures. He informed her that Striker's signal could come at any time and that she would be summoned immediately to join him on his next trip back in time.

Michele gave Bob a look of concern that he had not previously seen. He tried to reassure her that everything would work out, but his own doubts surfaced.

"Before your arrival my life was moving in a positive direction. Now I don't see my cat, Sheba, I'm living in a safehouse and my career is in the toilet."

"Would you rather I'd keep you out of this and not contact you again, Michele?"

"No, that's not it. I'm just frustrated. I want so much to bust Striker and Otto and help you too."

After a lengthy discussion Michele's attitude changed. She calmed down and even her body language became more open. Bob could not block out the sexual thoughts he had about her and his desire to get to know her better on all levels. Their discussion took a different path.

"Most people are so worried about getting what they need, they don't go after what they want," Bob stated.

"And what do you want, Bob?" asked Michele.

"The same thing you want," declared Bob.

"And what's that?"

"To find my soulmate," Bob responded.

Their eyes meet. He smiled at her. They both nodded to show that the feeling was mutual. Bob moved closer to her and was about to kiss Michele when suddenly he pulled back. They both felt somewhat ashamed and immediately changed the content of their discussion to return to the mission at hand.

It was Michele who finally broke the ice of their momentary silence.

"One thing I don't get, Bob, is why things haven't changed in our world considering the ripple point Striker created. I spent some time this afternoon doing historical and political research."

"And what did you discover?"

"That's it. Nothing has changed. The world that exists right now appears to be just the same as it was the day we left for New York in 1780.

"And this surprises you?"

"Of course it does. I'm no expert on the space-time continuum. Even I know that if you change a major event, like the Americans losing the Revolutionary War, that many changes should be seen over 200 years later."

"That would be correct if we were in the same universe, Michele, but we're not."

"What do you mean 'the same universe'?"

"You see, when a chrononaut travels back in time he or she does not arrive in the same exact universe they started out in."

"How is that possible, Bob?"

"We end up in a parallel universe, which is slightly

different from the one we left."

"Oh, I can see I'm in for another lecture on hyper-space physics. I need coffee. Would you like a cup?"

"No thanks."

When Michele returned she took a seat on the couch, kicked off her shoes and settled in for a long talk. The conversation eventually drifted towards a discussion of parallel universes. Bob began his explanation.

"According to well-established models of quantum physics, information is simultaneously flowing from the past to the future and from the future to the past. None of this information or choices (parallel universes) exist until we observe them. It is these quantum waves that carry this information to an infinite number of parallel universes."

"But Bob, just where are these parallel universes?"

"To comprehend this concept, consider all of our parallel selves in the same 'location' at the same 'time.' This is a type of hologram. Each parallel universe is simply a characteristic, or optional path, of our five-dimensional being. Think of a past or future event in our current parallel universe of frequency (the one that we are aware of at this moment) as part of history (existing in simultaneous time) and a component of probable parallel universes (never ending, as we continually create additional universes). Each and every one of these parallel universes contain yous and mes superimposed upon each other."

"Can you give me a simple example of how this works?" Michele inquired.

"The field of quantum mechanics, or quantum

physics as it is most commonly called, states that a flipped coin lands either heads up or tails up, but never heads and tails up simultaneously. For each statistical possibility there exists a parallel universe in which that particular potentiality becomes actual reality."

"Are you saying that both events occur, Bob?"

"Exactly. In one universe the coin lands heads up, while in the other it lands tails up. Even more interesting is that you occupy both universes observing the outcome. You exist in each separate universe at once, yet there is no direct bridge between the two; the complementary worlds remain hidden from one another. Your existence spans all the parallel universes simultaneously. Parallel universes are predicted by both quantum theory and Einstein's theory of relativity."

"When did all this theorizing occur, Bob?"

"It all began at Princeton University in 1957 when a graduate student in quantum mechanics named Hugh Everett III mathematically demonstrated that there are parallel universes. He obtained his doctorate on what he termed the 'Many worlds interpretation of quantum mechanics.'"

"How was his theory received?"

"Not well. According to Everett each of these universes was constantly splitting, resulting in an infinite number of parallel universes. Even though his evaluations held up, most physicists rejected this theory and still do in 2005."

"Has anyone ever disputed this parallel universe theory?"

"No. You see when the superstring theory was

proposed in the late 1960s to attempt to explain our universe, physicists realized that the three dimensions of length, width and depth weren't enough. Time is added as the fourth dimension to this paradigm. In reality, time is the fourth dimension of the space-time continuum. To our concept of existence we must now add a fifth dimension of parallel lives occurring on parallel universes, as well as hyperspace in general."

"What about the M-theory that I keep reading about?"

"In M-theory the universe is composed of eleven dimensions with ten dimensions of space and one dimension of time. This would conflict with parallel universes in which different events occur during the same time in sister universes."

"Doesn't M-theory nullify Everett's work?"

"Not really, because of the F-theory. In F-theory the universe consists of twelve dimensions, two dimensions of time and ten dimensions of space. This extra time dimension allows for different events in the parallel universe to take place at the exact same time our universe is existing."

"Bob, I read about parallel universes in the August 2000 issue of *Scientific American* titled 'The Universe's Unseen Dimensions.' In the article scientists state, 'Parallel universes may exist invisibly along ours, on their own membranes less than a millimeter away from ours,'" Michele read from her issue of this magazine.

"That's quite correct. Our universe is considered by scientists to be one bubble among an infinite number of membranous bubbles which ripple through a quantum foam as they move through the twelve dimensions. Remember, a millimeter is 1/1000 of 39.37 inches."

"What about UFOs? How do they fit into the theory?"

"I surely don't have to tell you that there are many reports of UFOs by police officers, pilots, air traffic controllers, meteorologists and other trained observers. These reports can not be explained away as plasma ball lightning, Venus or swamp gas. The spontaneous appearance and disappearance of UFOs finds resolutions in the parallel universe model, which accounts for their sudden arrivals and departures in terms of instantaneous shifts between worlds. The very craft piloted by Striker to come to 1999 would be labeled as a UFO."

"Could you explain how parallel universes explain time travel, Bob?"

"All futures and pasts exist concurrently. Time is not so much a river flowing past our vantage point, of which only a fraction is discernible at any one juncture, but rather is like a huge ocean that we can take in with a single glance. If quantum waves are the actual medium of thought, could they not travel outward or inward, passing through the nearest black hole into parallel universe that may exist in our past or future? Surely, if thoughts were superluminal and were carried by quantum waves, they could travel to the edge of the universe and back almost instantaneously. (Based on the computed density of quantum foam, namely 3.6×10^{93} g/cm^3, the round trip would take only 10^{78} seconds!) Signals traveling this fast could be 'reflected' backward in time."

"This quantum theory seems so hard for the

average person to comprehend," Michele exclaimed.

"We can use the common examples of computer chips and supermarket scanners to see quantum theory in our everyday life. This just reinforces the fact that quantum theory gives us an accurate description of the universe."

"So Bob if Striker created ripple points in a parallel universe, why should we care? After all, it doesn't affect us, does it?"

"Unfortunately it does. You see when we travel back in time we actually visit a sister universe. In the multi-universe aspect of our world the universes are splitting repeatedly. There are many newly created universes that are quite similar to ours. It is these similar universes that interact with us."

"So what about the ripple points Striker created?"

"These ripple points created in the parallel universes are exerting apocalyptic effects in our present universe in the 36th-century due to this interaction."

"Oh, now I get it. We are all in deep doodoo, huh?"

"Not all, just the universes similar to the one Striker went to. That includes this one."

Bob then described in detail Nova's report of events that were taking place in the 36th-century. Michele sat there with a look of horror as he detailed the apocalyptic scenes of his century.

In the 13th-century B.C. in what is known as Israel today, the Ark of the Covenant was jealously guarded by the Hebrews now engaged in a war with the Philistines. But the tide has turned and the Philistines conquered the

Hebrews and carried off the Ark of the Covenant as a token of conquest. The Ark was placed in the temple of the fish-god Dagon at Ashdod. Shortly thereafter the statue of Dagon falls and breaks. The people of Ashdod are plagued by disease and the Ark is eventually returned to the Hebrews.

Moses has died and Joshua is the Hebrew leader. The Hebrews' goal is the subjugation of the promised land. Their main foe was a new people called Philistines who were settling along the coast in a series of cities, such as Gaza, Gath, Ashdod, Ashkelon and Ekron.

The Hebrews faced the Philistines in possession of the fertile lowlands of the south and the Canaanites and Phoenicians holding out against the Israelites in the north.

Bob's teleporter now informed him that Striker teleported back to 1275 B.C. Israel. Nova's robot was immediately notified and research material, clothing and other aids were teleported to Bob.

Eleven

Bob and Michele had quite a bit to think about. Both of them were failing in their respective assignments. It's one thing to be chewed out by your boss, but when the fate of the galaxy is at risk, the stakes are enormous.

Then there was the issue of the growing sexual tension between them. Both of them felt this strong urge, but neither could do anything about it. It was a constant form of uneasiness that added to their stress.

Although the year 2005 was not affected by Striker's ripple points, Bob's time in the 36th-century most certainly was. He kept records of all his communications with Nova and reviewed the last two carefully. It unnerved him to see holographic images of his world literally coming apart.

Now Michele was to join him again on a trip back in time. She had no chrononaut training and this concerned Bob. On the plus side Michele was bright and resourceful. She could be a great help to him.

"Bob, did Nova send you the research you requested yet?"

"Yes and the clothing too. There is quite a bit of material here. We will have to leave soon, so I'm going to give you a brief summary of the era and what I think Striker is up to."

Bob began a long briefing describing the history of the Jewish civilization and the importance of the Ark of the Covenant. "The country of Israel lies between the Mediterranean to the west and a desert beyond Jordan to the east. Its location on a trade route between the Hittites, Syria, Assyria, Babylonia to the north and Egypt to the south led to a history of wars for power.

"The Old Testament details a history of the founders of the Hebrew nation, Abraham, Isaac and Jacob. The God of Abraham promises him and his people the land occupied by the Canaanites (Palestine today), called the land of milk and honey."

"Joshua becomes the Hebrew leader following the death of Moses and conquers Jericho, thus defeating the Canaanites. This success is not repeated in subsequent books of the Bible and the Jewish people lose heart, desert their God and worship Baal and Asharoth. Their people mix with the Philistines, Hittites and others.

"Under a series of wise men and heroes they wage more failed attempts at conquest and are conquered by the Moabites, Canaanites, Midianites and Philistines. We learn from the first Book of Samuel the value of the Ark of the Covenant.

And when the Ark of the Covenant of the Lord
came into the camp, all Israel shouted with a great shout,
so that the Earth rang again. And when the Philistines
heard the noise of the shout, they said, "What meaneth
the noise of this great shout in the camp of the
Hebrews?" And they understood that the Ark of the Lord
was come into the camp. And the Philistines were afraid,
for they said, "God is come into the camp." And they
said, "Woe unto us for there hath not been such a thing
heretofore. Woe unto us! who shall deliver us out of the
hand of these mighty Gods? These are the Gods that
smote the Egyptians with all the plagues in the
wilderness. Be strong, and quit yourselves like men, O
ye Philistines, that ye be not servants unto the Hebrews,
as they have been to you: quit yourselves like men, and
fight."

And the Philistines fought, and fought, heroically.
"Israel was smitten, and they fled every man into his tent:
and there was a very great slaughter, for there fell of
Israel thirty thousand footmen. And the Ark of God was
taken; and the two sons of Eli, Hophni and Phinehas,
were slain.

And there ran a man of Benjamin out of the army,
and came to Shiloh the same day, with his clothes rent,
and with earth upon his head. And when he came, lo, Eli
sat upon a seat by the wayside watching: for his heart
trembled for the Ark of God. And when the man came
into the city, and told it, all the city cried out. And when
Eli heard the noise of the crying, he said, "What meaneth
the noise of this tumult?" And the man came in hastily,
and told Eli. Now Eli was ninety and eight years old; and

his eyes were dim that he could not see. And the man said unto Eli, "I am he that came out of the army, and I fled to-day out of the army." And he said, "What is there done, my son?" And the messenger answered and said, "Israel is fled before the Philistines, and there hath been also a great slaughter among the people, and thy two sons also, Hophni and Phinehas, are dead, and the Ark of God is taken." And it came to pass, when he made mention of the Ark of God, that Eli fell from the seat backward, by the side of the gate, and his neck broke, and he died: for he was an old man, and heavy. And he had judged Israel forty years.

"Samuel was the last of the judges and the successor to Eli. Saul became their first king and was killed in Mount Gilboa by the Philistines. David replaced Saul and his son Solomon followed David as the Hebrew monarch.

"It is Solomon who ordered the construction of an elaborate temple. Prior to this the Ark was kept in a large tent, which had been shifted from one high place to another, and sacrifices had been offered to the God of Israel upon a number of different high places. Now the Ark is brought into the golden splendours of the inner chamber of a temple of cedar-sheathed stone, and put between two great winged figures of gilded olivewood, and sacrifices are henceforth to be made only upon the altar before it.

"The brief glory of the Hebrew nation ended with the death of Solomon. The Jews were later conquered by the Assyrians, Persians, Babylonians, Greeks and Romans. We find in the Old Testament the idea of a saviour, or Messiah, who would realize the long-ago promises of the God of Abraham. The Hebrew belief in one God is a parallel development of the free consciousness of mankind. There now runs through human thought a promise of the possibility of an active peace and happiness in human affairs.

"The importance of Judaism is reflected in the rise of Christianity. Jesus arose from the line of David and over two billion people today follow his religion. The other well-known monotheistic religion of Islam was founded by the prophet Mohammad and has as its basis the Old Testament's story of Abraham and his servant Hagar.

"So each of the three major monotheistic religions we see today owe their existence to the Old Testament and the Ark of the Covenant."

"That's all fine, Bob, but what about the Ark itself? How did it fit in with the history of the Jews?"

With this query Bob continued his briefing now focusing in on the Ark of the Covenant. "The Ark of the Covenant was a kind of chest, measuring two cubits and a half in length, a cubit and a half in breadth, and a cubit and a half in height.

"It was constructed from shittimwood and overlaid with pure gold. There was a gold crown or rim around it. Four golden rings at the corners were placed so that two bars of shittimwood (overlaid with gold) could be used to carry the Ark. The propitiatory, or cover, was made also of pure gold. Upon the propitiatory was placed two cherubim of beaten gold, looking towards each other, and spreading their wings so that both sides of the propitiatory were covered.

"The Jewish law written by Moses was placed in the Ark. Moses was ordered by God to put into the tabernacle near the Ark the reed of Aaron and a golden vessel holding a gomor of manna."

"Isn't it ironic that Striker's head of Mannaco is now out to destroy the Ark that contains the very essence of his success in 2005?" Michele commented.

"I could say that the Lord works in mysterious ways, but that would be trite. In Numbers we read that when Moses entered into the tabernacle of the covenant to consult God, he heard the voice of God speaking to him from the propitiatory that was over the Ark between the two cherubims.

"The Ark represented God's presence in the midst of His people. No greater evil could befall the Hebrew people than the capture of the Ark by their enemies. This sacred chest also was the visible sign of God's protection.

A good example of this is in the Book of Joshua (iii, 14-17)

"The priests that carried the Ark of the Covenant went on before them, and as soon as they came into the Jordan, and their feet were dipped in part of the water, the waters that came down from above stood in one place, and swelling up like a mountain, were seen afar off...but those that were beneath ran down from the sea of the wilderness, until they wholly failed. And the people marched over against Jericho; and the priests that carried the Ark of the Covenant of the Lord, stood girded upon the dry ground, in the midst of the Jordan, and all the people passed over through the channel that was dried.

"A few days later, Israel was besieging Jericho. At God's command, the Ark was carried in procession around the city for seven days, until the walls crumbled at the sound of the trumpets and the shouts of the people, thus giving the assailing army a free opening into the place.

"One final story of the Ark's significance took place following the Hebrew conquering of Jericho. After the Philistines defeated the Israelites in battle, the Jewish priests suggested that the Ark be brought out to save them from their enemy. The Ark was removed from Silo and brought to the camp of the Israelites. The Hebrews were again defeated and the Philistines confiscated the Ark.

"In the opinion of the Philistines, the taking of the Ark meant a victory of the gods over the God of Israel. They brought it to Azotus and set it as a trophy in the temple of Dagon. But the next morning they found Dagon fallen upon his face before the Ark. They raised him up and set him in his place again. The following morning Dagon again was lying on the ground badly mutilated. At the same time a cruel disease killed the Azotites, while a terrible invasion of mice afflicted the whole surrounding country. These scourges were soon attributed to the presence of the Ark within the walls of the city, and regarded as a direct judgment from Yahweh. It was decided by the assembly of the rulers of the Philistines that the Ark should be removed from Azotus and brought to some other place. It was then taken to Gath and to Accaron. The Ark brought with it the same scourges which had occasioned its removal from Azotus. Finally, after seven months, on the suggestion of their priests and their diviners, the Philistines resolved to give up their trophy and returned the Ark to the Hebrews."

As Bob concluded his discussion Michele sat for a few moments to digest it all. She scratched her head and blew the bangs out of her eyes and continued with her questions.

"Why do you think Striker chose 1275 B.C.?" she asked.

"The only strategy I can think of is the battle of Jericho. After traveling in the Sinai desert the Jews wanted a homeland. Moses had died and Joshua was his chosen successor. Joshua's successful campaign in conquering the Canaanites and taking Jericho fulfilled the promise God made to Abraham five centuries earlier. If Striker could somehow prevent this conquest and destroy the Ark, he could create the very ripple point he needs to effect his plan of destroying our galaxy."

Back in Calabasas Otto was bored. He had been stuck in Striker's house for days with nothing to do. His boss was gone and "cabin fever" has tempted Otto to go out for the evening.

He drove out to a club in Sherman Oaks that he had heard of but never been to before. As he entered the club Otto scanned the bar for people who might recognize him. The last thing he needed now was to alert any police or other enemies as to his presence.

Otto saw no one he knew so he walked over to the bar and sat next to an attractive young brunette. She wore heavy makeup, her face a flawless cosmetic mask.

Otto's attention was focused on her white dress, full-skirted so that he was aware of her thighs and body moving under the thin material when she left to go to the ladies room.

His look must have been transparent as she never returned. Otto looked around the bar and spotted a redhead with a slender, rather elegant nose. She appeared to be in her late thirties, slim and attractive. He approached her trying to be cool.

"Say, are you a regular here?"

"No. I'm in town attending a sales conference and I'm rather bored," she responded.

"I'm just bored," Otto added.

"You seem like a guy who can take care of yourself. Are you a professional athlete?"

"No, just a bodyguard in need of a little excitement."

"I see you're not drinking. Are you a recovering alcoholic?"

"No. I just ordered a Scotch and soda. It will be here shortly."

Otto did notice the tall, athletic young man with a sandy mustache, rugged good looks, brown hair and a cell phone observing him from a distant table. He quickly called out to a car in the parking lot of the club. Within two minutes two thugs enter, their weapons ready, and joined the young man who pointed Otto out to them.

"Put those guns away, you jerks. Go up to him and lead him out into the alley now," ordered the young man.

As the two thugs approached the bar, Otto was

busy with his conversation with the redhead.

"Remember Pasquale DeNardo from New York?" one of the thugs asked Otto as he shoved the gun butt into Otto's back.

"Put that away. You guys don't want to kill me. I can lead you to Striker," Otto begged.

"Our orders are to kill you. Make it easy on yourself and get up now," demanded one of the thugs.

Otto used all his skills and wielded his body around, grabbing the thug's gun and hitting him over the head. This thug fell to the ground as the other thug dove under a nearby table. Otto fired the gun he grabbed from the first thug, aiming at the thug under the table. This thug was hit in the foot and screamed in agony.

Otto now ran away from the bar and fired again at the thug under the table, hitting him in the chest. The eyes of this thug went cold and lifeless as he died.

Suddenly, the windows splintered with the sound of a silenced automatic weapon, as the first thug whom Otto hit regained consciousness from the blow with the gun Otto had wrestled from the thug. Otto scrambled across the room and fired back as he ran out the door, being chased by bullets.

Otto was fortunate to have parked his Jaguar right in front of the club. He jumped in his car and headed for the Ventura Freeway. The other thug eventually got into his car, trying to follow Otto.

The police were called and Otto now had two problems. He must elude the DeNardo thug and not allow himself to be stopped by the police. His arrest warrant would automatically place him in federal custody.

As he drove on the freeway Otto noted headlights flashing across his face in a continuous, hypnotic rhythm. He got off the freeway at the Calabasas exit and made it back to Striker's house. A misty fog settled over the ground. Otto made his way to his room. He was exhausted, and his clothes were soaked with sweat. It will be awhile until he ventures out of the house again.

Bob decided that he and Michele should teleport to 1276 B.C. one year earlier than Striker. This way they could get a feel as to the territory and trace the route of the Hebrews and the Ark.

"Why are we going back so early, Bob?"

"This mission is far too important. We can always jump to 1275 B.C., but we still can't pinpoint Striker's precise location. It's best to simply follow the Ark."

It is impossible to describe the awe of witnessing history in the making. This especially applies to religious history if you follow that particular theology. Michele is a Christian and firmly believes in both the Old and New Testaments. So when she observed Moses enter the tabernacle to communicate with God by way of the Ark, she was speechless. The following is what she and Bob heard being transmitted from the Ark:

"Behold, I make a covenant: before all thy people I will do marvels, such as have not been done in all the earth, nor in any nation; and all the people among which thou art shall see the work of the Lord....

"Observe thou that which I command thee this day: behold, I drive out before thee the Amorite, and the Canaanite, and the Hittite, and the Perizite, and the

Hivite, and the Jebusite."

As the wandering Jews continued their trip through the wilderness, a small army of Amorites numbering several thousand men began to attack them. Moses ordered Joshua to prepare the soldiers for battle.

Bob explained to Michele that Joshua's position with the Hebrews grew in importance throughout their forty years in the desert. Joshua functioned as a spy, an assistant to Moses, a warrior and finally as Moses' designated successor.

Joshua assembles the men and just prior to joining the Amorites in battle, the Levi priests bring out the Ark and say:

"Arise, O Lord, and let thy enemies be scattered, and let them that hate thee flee from before thy face."

The battle was joined and the Hebrew warriors led by Joshua easily won. The Amorites that survived scattered into the desert never to bother these people again. Following the battle the Levi priests again brought out the Ark, set it down and uttered:

"Return, o Lord, to the multitude of the host of Israel."

Bob and Michele observed this scene from the fifth dimension and were silent for several minutes. They then returned to the three-dimensional world to plan their next move.

"Bob, that was amazing. What are your plans now?"

"Let's continue to follow the Ark and observe its path by way of the fifth dimension. Remember, you and I can see each other and can communicate with each other easily because of our close location."

"Can't we spot Striker if he is also observing the Ark from the fifth dimension?"

"No. There are simply too many corridors of the fifth dimension for him to hide in. We will have to stop him when he returns to the three-dimensional world and that always presents problems."

"How so?"

"You see, Striker knows exactly where he wants to go and we can't trace him. His timeliner status from the 21st-century makes it impossible for my equipment to tag him."

"Can you explain what just happened with Moses and the Ark?"

"According to the Old Testament the Lord gave the tribe of Levi the responsibility to guard the Ark and to bless it in his name. When Moses went into the tabernacle of the congregation to speak with God, he heard God's voice speaking to him from the mercy seat that was located between the two cherubims on top of the Ark."

"Wow," Michele exclaimed.

"Now let me review the events of the battle of Jericho so we are both on the same page, so to speak. In 1275 B.C. Moses had died and Joshua was now the leader of the Israelites. They were stationed on the eastern bank of the Jordan River, just north of the Dead Sea. Joshua sent spies across the Jordan to survey the situation. When the presence of these Hebrews was detected, a Canaanite woman, Rahab the harlot, befriended them. She saved their lives and the spies promised that she and her family would be spared during the coming invasion."

"Was this plan devised by Joshua?" she asked.

"No. This was God's plan as he communicated it to Joshua. The Hebrews were to encompass the walls of the city once a day for six days, then seven times on the seventh day. A blast was to be made on the priests' trumpets, the people were to give a great shout, and the city would be theirs. When the Hebrew people followed this plan, the walls of Jericho fell down. The Israelites then destroyed the inhabitants of the city (with the exception of Rahab and her family). They were charged to confiscate the gold and silver and the vessels of brass and iron for the Lord's treasury, but they were prohibited from taking any personal booty. The city was then burned. Finally, a prophetic curse was placed upon any who attempted to refortify Jericho."

After this explanation Michele considered all the elements of the upcoming battle.

"Bob, if I remember my reading of the Book of Joshua, Jericho was strongly fortified and the attack took place in the spring after harvest time."

"That's correct."

"So militarily Striker would have a tough time upsetting history. I mean weren't there something like 40,000 Hebrew warriors engaged in this battle?"

"Yes, something like that. You see, the only real way Striker can succeed is to somehow capture and destroy the Ark. That would undoubtedly demoralize the Jews and create the ripple point he so desires."

"We must protect the Ark at all costs," Michele

commented.

"Yes. Remember, we are in a parallel universe to the one we both came from. Events here do interact with ours, so it is crucial that we succeed. If Striker beats us here our galaxy is doomed."

"Is the Ark of the Covenant that important, Bob? It's been lost to history and the three major monotheistic religions it is based on have survived and thrived."

"We have to consider the concept of hero worship in 2005. In your time the objects of hero worship are usually popular music, film, and sports stars, but in ancient times they tended to be kings, conquerors, and tribal leaders. It was common among ancient peoples to regard the ruler as a kind of god. The problem with hero worship is that you focus on their strengths and cannot see their weaknesses.

"The writers of the Old Testament were very much aware of the dangers of hero worship. Since the religion of the Hebrews was based on monotheism, or belief in one God, there could be only one fit object of worship: God Himself. The tendency to worship earthly kings, even worthy ancestors, left the way open to polytheism and idolatry. In the Old Testament, only God is faultless. Every human personality—even the greatest of the Israelites—is shown to have human failings.

"Consider these examples. Adam and Eve, regarded by the Bible as our first parents, are created by God in His own image, but their disobedience leads to their expulsion from the Garden of Eden and to a curse on all mankind. Noah is called a just man and perfect in his generation. God chooses him to build the ark that will protect a remnant of God's creation from the coming flood. Later, when the flood waters have subsided, Noah will become a winemaker, and his sons will find him lying naked and drunk. Moses, chosen by God to bring freedom and law to the children of Israel, is not permitted to enter the Promised Land because he disobeys a divine command in one of his typical displays of anger."

"And the significance of the Ark?"

"Michele, without the Ark the Old Testament would never have survived. Consider that the Old Testament presents each character as worthy to the extent that he follows the ways of God, and as flawed to the extent that he substitutes his own desires for the divine will. Without the Old Testament there would be no monotheistic religions and polytheism and idolatry would have dominated civilization. Even in this parallel universe, the ripple point created would have enormous effects on our universe."

As Bob and Michele continue their conversation they are unaware of an important event taking place several months forward in time from where they are now. Striker has entered the three dimensional world and has decided to kill one of the Hebrews to take his clothes so that he can blend in with the rest of Joshua's men.

Striker patiently waited for one of the Jews to become isolated. This Hebrew was approximately the same size as he, so he attacked him. The Hebrew was much stronger than Striker assumed and a lengthy fight ensued. During the struggle the warrior knocked Striker's phaser against a rock just as Striker was about to kill him with it.

Striker was now livid with anger and tackled the Hebrew with such a force that the warrior's head smashes against another rock and the Hebrew died. Now Striker removed the dead Hebrew's clothes and puts them on. He teleported his old clothes and the dead Jew into the fifth dimension and joined the rest of Joshua's men.

When Striker joined the camp of over 40,000 Hebrews, he is not noticed. The special morphing device he brought from the 36th-century allowed him to alter his physical appearance so he looked just like any other Hebrew. He overheard Joshua addressing his men.

"Prepare your victuals, for within three days ye shall pass over this Jordan, to go in to possess the land, which the Lord your God giveth you to posses it," Joshua commands.

"Wherever you commandest us Joshua, we will go," responded one of his men.

"When ye see the Ark of the Covenant of the Lord your God, and the priests the Levites bearing it, then ye shall remove from your place and go after it. There shall be a space between you and it, about two thousand cubits by measure. Come not near unto it," directed Joshua.

As Striker observes this scene, he is not in awe. He is rather frustrated. All he can focus on now is how he can capture and destroy the Ark. His phaser is useless. Fortunately, his teleporter wasn't damaged during his struggle with the warrior he killed, or he would have been stranded in 1275 B.C. He knew that if Bob saw him he would not recognize the morphed Striker. A new plan had to be devised and fast.

Bob and Michele now teleported to 1275 B.C. and

arrived at Joshua's camp on the eastern bank of the Jordan River. From the fifth dimension they both overheard Joshua ordering two of his men to spy.

"Go view the land, even Jericho," Joshua commanded.

"Michele, I would like you to stand guard over the Ark with your phaser while I follow the two spies. Be wary of Striker. He probably has morphed his appearance, so you won't recognize him physically. Remember, his phaser is just as powerful as yours."

Bob was not aware of his good fortune. He would have been more confident of this mission had he known that Striker's phaser was useless. The two spies Joshua sent to Jericho found lodging at the house of a harlot named Rahab. Bob followed them in the fifth dimension keeping a lookout for anyone trying to sabotage this mission. He knew that could only be Striker.

Shortly after the spies arrived at Rahab's house, the king of Jericho discovered the presence of the spies and confronted Rahab. She was questioned about the spies and denied seeing them. Just prior to the king's visit, Rahab hid the two spies on the roof of her family's home under stallics of flax. The king appeared satisfied and left her house.

She now went to the roof and told the spies that they were safe and could escape to rejoin their troops.

"I know that the Lord hath given you the land. We have heard how the Lord dried up the water of the Red Sea for you when ye came out of Egypt. I pray you, since I have shown you kindness, that ye shall also show kindness to my father's house," begged Rahab.

"If ye utter not our business it shall be," responded one of the spies.

Bob was pleased with what he observed because he knew this was the historical account as recorded in the Old Testament. He followed the two spies back to Joshua's camp.

"Truly the Lord hath delivered into our hands all the land," one of the spies declared to Joshua.

Joshua retired to his tent and now briefed his generals as to the battle plan. Bob returned and met with Michele. He cautioned her to be vigilant.

"Striker is here somewhere Michele. He most likely is hiding out in the fifth dimension, but can appear at any moment to attack the Ark."

"Don't worry, Bob. I will be an extra pair of eyes for you. I know how to handle myself if I run into Striker."

As Bob and Michele watched over the camp and the 40,000 Hebrew warriors preparing for battle, they were on the lookout for Striker. They did not see any suspicious person, but continued a constant watch.

They both heard Joshua giving final orders to his generals.

"Only Rahab the harlot and all that are with her in the house shall live, because she hid the messengers that we sent," instructed Joshua.

Over the next six days at dawn the Hebrew army surrounded the city of Jericho and then returned to the camp. There was very little fighting at the time. It was a routine that Bob and Michele observed carefully. There still was no sign of Striker.

Bob and Michele knew that Striker was going to act soon. The Hebrew instructions from God was to now surround the city of Jericho several times on the seventh day. Then the priests would blast their trumpets and all would shout as the walls of Jericho would crumble.

While in our three-dimensional world dressed in the clothing of the times, Bob and Michele blended in with the Jewish people. Bob stood near the Ark while Michele milled around looking for a suspicious man she would assume would be Striker.

She took a break and sat by a rock, thinking about this crucial mission when suddenly someone grabbed her from behind and hit her on the back of the head with a block of wood. Michele fell to the ground in a dazed state and could barely make out the figure standing above her.

The first thing she observed was that it was Striker. He had morphed back to his regular appearance and stood above her holding her phaser.

"I have to thank you Special Agent Peterman for giving me the equipment I need to complete my plan," Striker gloated.

"What do you mean?" Michele asked.

"During a struggle with the previous occupant of these clothes my phaser was damaged, and as I fear, beyond repair. That means I had no easy way to destroy the Ark."

"Now you do."

"Yes. Thanks to your momentary blackout I now have your phaser. I will kill you in just a few moments, but before you die I want you to know my plan and to curse yourself throughout eternity for being responsible for the destruction of the galaxy."

"You know, Striker, that you are one sick megalomaniac," Michele retorted.

"I may be sick by your cop definition, but it is I with the upper hand. Now say your prayers Miss FBI."

Suddenly, a phaser shot blew a cloud of smoke at Striker's feet. He immediately teleported into the fifth dimension carrying Michele's phaser with him. Michele looked around and now with a clear head could see Bob approaching rapidly.

"I'm sorry I didn't get here sooner. When I observed that man stalking you I figured it must be Striker," Bob remarked.

"You are correct. It was Striker. He can morph his appearance and now has my phaser."

Michele briefed Bob about Striker's remarks and how she indirectly supplied him with the means to complete his plan.

"Don't be so hard on yourself. We all make mistakes. If my shot killed him we both would have succeeded. Let's regroup and focus on tomorrow's activities."

Bob and Michele both realized that destroying the Ark would have a greater effect on demoralizing the Jews if Striker could somehow show that it failed to win the upcoming battle.

At dawn on the following day the Hebrew warriors surrounded the walls of Jericho and returned to camp. Then they repeated this activity a second, third, fourth, fifth and sixth time as God had instructed. Nothing unusual happened.

Bob and Michele were now more than ever on the lookout for Striker. He most likely would strike at any time. Joshua's men removed the Ark from the tabernacle and brought it with them for the seventh and final encompassing of Jericho.

Little did the Jewish army realize that two of the people with them were time travelers. As the soldiers were surrounding the walls of Jericho for the seventh time, the Levi priests lifted the Ark and declared:

"Arise O Lord and let they enemies be scattered, and let them that hate thee flee from before thy face!"

The Levi priests then placed the Ark down gently to the ground and lifted their trumpets. As they blasted their trumpets a luminescent white image suddenly appeared in front of the Ark and declared:

"People of Israel, you have disappointed me for the last time. I hereby abandon you now and forever."

With that declaration Striker masquerading as God fired his phaser at the Ark and watched it erupt in a circle of flames and explode. Striker immediately teleported back to 2005 before either Bob or Michele could act.

As a result of Striker's masquerade the Hebrew soldiers scattered and dispersed back over the Jordan River. Joshua was killed by his own priests and there was no subsequent alliance with Gibeon or victories against Hoban, king of Hebron; Piram, king of Jarmuth; Japhia, king of Lachish; or Debir, king of Eglon.

There was no Hebrew nation of Israel and no Christianity or Islam. The world remained polytheistic and worshipped idols through the year 2005 in this parallel universe. The ripple point created was enormous in size.

In Nova's office a newscaster was seen via hologram. This female reporter was losing the fight to control her emotions. She pointed up at a giant vortex swirling in the sky like a giant whirlpool, sucking everything up around it, and announced:

"Scientists are still at a loss as to how to stop the vortex from consuming the entire solar system. They say it's as if the space-time continuum has been ripped apart. Everything is being destroyed. It's the end of time. This is the Apocalypse."

Twelve

Drax received another report regarding the three ripple points created by Striker and smiled wryly. He stared out of his window and contemplated what the universe will be like following the destruction of our galaxy.

"Striker, you don't realize how happy you are making me. What you don't know is your own fate. When you arrive here I will personally show you the destruction of your galaxy and then slowly kill you. You fool. Ha, ha, ha, ha!!!" Drax yelled at the top of his lungs without the benefit of an audience.

Back in Woodland Hills Bob received an emergency hologram from Nova.

"Bob, we're in deep trouble. I'm communicating with you from an underground shelter. Most of our top government agents and representatives have moved underground." Nova was very emotional as she described the current state of affairs.

"What's happening on the surface, Nova?"

"For example, the Golden Gate Bridge has been pulled to pieces. Panic and terror has gripped everyone on the planet. The black hole is much larger and the world is in peril."

"I have failed you Nova, but all is not lost," Bob frowned perplexedly.

"Look, Bob, I know you've done your best, but the entire planet is being torn apart in an apocalyptic destruction. The rest of the galaxy will follow."

"Nova our one hope is patching the space-time continuum."

"Bob, using the time sequence nullification unit is for minor ripple points. It has never been applied for a tear this large. It simply won't work."

"Look, Nova, we have no other options. I have been working on a method to expand the patching function of the time sequence nullification unit (TSNU)."

"What do you need from me, Bob?"

"Teleport me a TSNU and some exotic matter and some additional equipment listed on the computer chip I'm sending you. Michele and I will begin the patching as soon as I receive the equipment."

"Because of my underground location it may take a few hours to get you the equipment. I will see to it that you receive it pronto."

Bob knew Nova was upset and that time was working against him. Whenever Nova failed to refer to him as hotshot, he knew he was in trouble. Now Bob had to brief Michele on his patching plan and prepare her for the most important mission a chrononaut has ever been assigned.

It was not easy to begin this briefing with Michele. Even though she was the only 21st-century citizen he could trust, this was one heck of a responsibility to place on someone.

"Michele, it will be a few hours before we begin a procedure known as patching. Do you have any questions about anything we're doing now?"

"Yes, Bob. I don't understand how you could have saved George Washington after he was dead if you did something to his body within an hour of his physical death."

"This requires an understanding of something called *intergalactic lines* (IL) and *quantum medicine.* Quantum medicine utilizes fifth-dimensional states of matter to alter magnetic fields. Think of the meridians of acupuncture as an example of this principle. An acupuncturist uses needles, or electricity combined with needles, to balance energy blocks along these meridians to effect healing.

"Humankind actually exists between magnetic grids delineated within our body and the universe's magnetic field as a whole. Our body is in reality a grid of magnetic fields tied together by intergalactic lines originating from the god energy complex and accessible to us by way of our Higher Self, which is the perfect component of our soul's energy.

"The ILs are part of a fifth-dimensional magnetic field which provides the basic energy used for renewing functions of the body. The IL can be used for the complete regeneration of an organ or limb and even to resurrect the dead. Our Higher Self receives the creative energy from the IL by way of connecting points in the universe called *conversion points*. These points admit sound and light vibrations that alter the spin of cell molecules to effect regeneration or restore life itself. These grids are organized to exchange genetic information and transmit your life force throughout the body through a network of messenger cells, which are passed on to any part of the body."

"Fascinating," exclaimed Michele. But aren't you playing God when you resurrect the dead?"

"Not really. Forget your religion for a moment. If man wasn't supposed to do this, there are plenty of forces in the universe that would have prevented us from developing this technology."

"OK, I think I understand quantum medicine. Now how about explaining teleportation."

"There is research going on today in 2005 regarding teleportation. In 1998 three different laboratories around the world demonstrated the teleportation of subatomic particles. These labs were located in Rome, Innsbruck, Austria and at Cal Tech in Pasadena, California.

"The problem with this research was that in order to teleport a human, you would have to destroy the person and transmit a duplicate of themselves from one location to another. In addition, the amount of memory storage for any such apparatus was enormous and far beyond anything that scientists of your time could create.

"It took 1,500 years for scientists to develop a fifth-dimensional computer chip which functions through a small device to enable us to teleport in time anywhere instantly. We do not dematerialize and rematerialize as was depicted on *Star Trek*. What we are doing is moving through hyperspace without causing tears in the fabric of space-time, as was created by enlarging wormholes. We are simply using quantum technology to manipulate coordinate changes in the multi-universe. Does that make sense to you, Michele?"

"I still don't comprehend all of this hyperspace physics, but I'll take your word for it. Now how about discussing parallel universes again and how this patching works."

"Parallel universes are simply sister universes that exist in the fifth dimension side by side with ours."

"How close are they to us?"

"According to the August 2000 issue of *Scientific American*, the closest sister universe is less than a millimeter away. That is less than 1/400 of an inch. When Hugh Everett III first demonstrated the mathematical model for parallel universes in 1957 in Princeton, he showed that the universe is constantly splitting.

"There are duplicates of you and me in each of these parallel universes, each of which functions on a different frequency. The exact outcome of these futures are different, depending on our actions and choices we make. Our consciousness can only recognize one frequency at a time. This is the reason you are not now aware of your other parallel selves in the present.

Since we now must deal with all possible parallel universes, a different type of space exists. The term *hyperspace* refers to anything beyond the four-dimensional universe, in which time is the fourth dimension of the space-time continuum. Hyperspace contains all of these parallel universes. This is where time travelers pass through on their path to the past or future."

"And the black hole problem?" she asked.

"A black hole represents the initial stage in the collapse of a star, in which matter is squeezed to produce a singularity. These singularities exist in the centers of black holes. The laws of physics go haywire here. The black hole traps everything including light within it. All physical quantities take on infinite values and there is a connection to other universes in this area through what is called a wormhole. For example, the Big Bang was one large singularity. We travel in time to the past, parallel universes and the future, when there is a jump through a singularity in the interior of a rotating black hole."

"I guess that makes sense, but how can we fix our currently broken universe?"

"The one saving grace we have is the interconnectedness of parallel universes. A quantum foam contains wormholes that function to connect any event with any other event. For example, each time we throw a rock in a lake to create ripples, ripples are simultaneously made in many similar universes, and subatomic particles of the water from these parallel universes interact with those of our universe to produce the pattern we observe."

"I like your lake ripple analogy, Bob, since we are dealing with ripple points in time. Are all of these parallel universe actions taking place at the same time as ours?"

"No, not all of them. Since some of these parallel universes exist at an earlier time, we can go back to them and alter events in their universe, which, in turn will affect events through this subatomic interaction principle."

"But wouldn't that lead to completely different futures? That's where I get confused Bob."

"According to Everett's many worlds interpretation of quantum mechanics theory, the events in these parallel universes can be and are quite different. For example, Striker killed George Washington in one parallel universe, but not in ours. Every time we travel back in time we actually go to a parallel universe, not our own. The problem is that the events in some of these universes still affect us. That is why there is a huge black hole in 3567."

"So explain patching again."

"Michele, when we go back in time to the three time periods when Striker successfully created ripple points, we will meet all of our parallel selves. It is our job to keep out of the way of our alternate selves in this parallel universe, but still prevent Striker from succeeding in his plans."

"But Bob, how will that help us here?"

"Even though we are traveling to a sister universe in which Striker succeeded, if we defeat him there those effects will interact with the actual parallel universe in which he was successful and eventually ours in a positive way."

"So that alone will correct the problem?"

"No. Even if we are successful in these three time periods, we still have to patch up the tears that have resulted in the fabric of space-time. That is why I have ordered the TSNU and exotic matter that is necessary for its activation."

"But Nova did not seem optimistic that this patching will work. Why?"

"The TSNU works on the parallel world gateway and it has only been successful in relatively minor tears in space-time. Nobody has ever created the huge tears Striker has done. I have experimented with making adjustments to the TSNU and I am confident we will be successful in repairing these tears."

"What will happen in 3567 if we are successful?" she asked.

"The events Nova is reporting will never have occurred. In other words, the 3567 I left will be exactly the same when I return. This is why Nova wants me to keep records of her transmissions. Without them, she would have no knowledge of the black hole, since it would never have been created and therefore cannot exist.

"Won't Striker know when we teleport back to these three time periods?"

No, he won't. He doesn't have the equipment I possess. I can trace his teleportation back in time, but he can't trace ours."

"What do you think he's up to now?"

"I guess he is celebrating his victories. He must make certain preparations before he can relocate to Drax's galaxy. He knows that my people will know when he returns. We don't know his precise method of transportation to Drax's galaxy. The teleporter he has is not designed to function the boundaries of our galaxy, so he has to make other arrangements and he will have to do that fast."

Striker pondered his success. If his plan worked he would use the Stargate, whose construction he supervised, to leave this galaxy and enter Drax's. This would be in advance of the destruction of Earth's galaxy.

Drax, during one of Striker's trips to the former's galaxy by way of the Thorne Stargate, devised this escape route for Striker.

"So would you like me to explain how the Stargate works?" Drax's condescending voice infuriated Striker.

"No, that's not necessary. I can build one of those in my sleep," Striker replied.

"Good. You can supervise the construction of the Stargate with my twelve engineers, I mean ambassadors," Drax laughed as he teased Striker.

Striker compared Drax's ambassadors to those of the 20th-century Soviet Union. The Russian ambassadors to foreign countries were actually KGB agents trained to spy for Mother Russia. Drax's ambassadors were engineers trained to construct and operate a Stargate.

"Where do you want this Stargate built, Drax?" Striker asked.

"I have done a lot of research and decided that the safest location for the Stargate is in the Himalayas in

Tibet. This represents one of the most isolated regions of Earth and its vast spiritual history makes it an ironic choice for your most traitorous departure, don't you agree, Striker?"

"Yes. I wholeheartedly agree and appreciate your sense of humor, Drax."

A Stargate is a device that creates an artificial wormhole, a time-dimensional doorway to the past or future. This round portal can instantaneously transport an object or person from one place in time or location to another. As one travels through this device, a sense of being contorted physically, along with an avalanche of geometric designs and mental images, dominates the experience. It's enough to drive one insane. This device discouraged all but the most fit and adventurous from utilizing this form of time travel.

The eighteen-foot diameter of the Stargate consists of an outer circle and an inner wheel. When the unit is turned on and set to a specific location and time, a slight rumble is felt. This rumble increases geometrically until the entire room in which it is located experiences an intense earthquake-like effect. The vortex of the Stargate glows and when its occupants reach their location, both the glowing and rumbling quickly subside. The individuals traveling through the Stargate are disoriented and require several minutes to return to normal functioning.

The Stargate contains a giant covering which closes very quickly over the gate when it is operational. Each occupant of the Stargate must have a small transmitter capable of sending a specific coded signal through the gate. The device is called a gate synchronizer (GS). Once the GS sends the appropriate coded signal, it is safe to pass through the Stargate at either the beginning or end of a trip. If an improper (or no) signal is sent, the traveler's molecules would not rematerialize and they would cease to exist.

Testing the Stargate was always an experience to be noted. All travelers were forbidden from taking any meals before the transit. This was due to the fact that such a trip resulted in repeated vomiting if there was any food in the stomach. These trips were known as Stargate jumps that pummeled and twisted the body with a barrage of energy. Most travelers landed on their stomach, which only heightened the tendency to vomit.

What the Stargate traveler is actually doing is traversing the wormhole between the two gateways and experiencing different dimensions of time and space resulting in unexplainable phenomena. An Earthling would describe it as going over Niagara Falls in a barrel.

Stargate travel is one way. A traveler cannot go through the gate, leave it open, and then step back through it. The gate has to be stopped and then restarted from the opposite planet in order to travel back to the other side.

Striker's mind now moved to the time when the twelve Reptilian ambassadors last visited Earth. He was in charge of them and convinced the Federation Agency that their stay should be extended indefinitely so he could eliminate the hostilities that existed between the two galaxies.

During their trip to the extreme outskirts of the Himalayas, they were confronted with a huge mountain range over which they had to climb and bring their equipment. Fortunately, the antigravity devices Striker "borrowed" made their task easier.

Thick layers of ice coated their path as they moved across a wide sun-drenched plateau. They moved through a tunnel of deep gorges that glistened with gigantic mirrors of ice. A mere six weeks after selecting the perfect cave, construction of the rogue Stargate was completed. This was a rogue Stargate, since the TTSA was not notified of its construction or location. The TTSA most certainty would not have approved such a project, as it represents a major security breach for the entire galaxy.

The cave housing the Stargate had a separate tunnel bored through it to add to its secure location. This tunnel was long and narrow, its ceiling lined with electric lamps. It vaguely resembled the gallery of a coal mine. This tunnel led to another large and wide inner cave that finally housed the Stargate.

Other tunnels were carved out of this cave to make it difficult for intruders to locate the Stargate. The convergences of these side tunnels became more frequent as the main tunnel became more serpentine.

As Striker and the Reptilian ambassadors approached the main chamber housing the Stargate, he could feel vibrations running through the stone floor. Each Reptilian was dressed in a formfitting coverall, light tan or cream-colored, with a kind of sleeveless black tunic, edged with various rich shades of brown.

Now Striker pointed to one of the Reptilian ambassadors who would test the Stargate unit. The ambassador sent the appropriate coded signal to Drax's planet through his GS and a subsonic rumble manifested through the cave. This low-level rumble vibrated the very walls of the cave and everything in it.

Slowly, the inner wheel began to move. Gleaming blasts of energy punctured the sweep of the gate's outer circle. The glowing vortex swirled but then steadied into a pulsating pattern of energy. The inner circle moved as each part of the coordinate was locked in. The entire energy level of the cave appeared to ratchet upward.

Strands of radiance, like slow-motion lightning bolts, projected from each of the locking points. They writhed across the eighteen-foot diameter of the Stargate, expanding until the whole circle was filled with an unearthly iridescence. Energy suddenly spewed outward, then was just as suddenly sucked in the opposite direction.

In what seemed like an eternity the bead ambassador's communicator flashed red. He started at Striker and cursed. The Reptilian who entered the Stargate didn't arrive and wasn't coming back.

Thirteen

Now it was Striker's time to curse. Something went very wrong with the Reptilian's GS. A signal was most definitely sent, but it obviously was not the correct signal. As a result the Reptilian traveler's molecules were vaporized and he no longer existed.

Striker and the head Reptilian went to work on the GS to fix this problem. They did not like each other and a battle of egos ensued.

"What do you mean it was my fault? You idiot, you programmed the GS," Striker barked at the head Reptilian.

"Look Striker, my programming was perfect. Something must have taken place during transit to this hole in the wall location in the middle of nowhere."

"Would you like me to relay that message to Drax? After all, he selected this place," responded Striker.

"We both know that a Stargate transfer with an appropriate GS coded signal to the unit on the receiving end is placed into a state of matter that is not a part of space as we normally know it. The receiving Stargate is placed in the same condition and tuning is accomplished once they are locked onto the same frequency," the Reptilian stated.

"Yes, and in a sense they become part of one another and the distance of the intervening space does not matter. If you step into one you will step out of the other without any awareness of either time or spatial separation," countered Striker.

"Some additional pressures between our galaxies apparently affected the very binding energy of the atoms. This Stargate is somewhat different than the other back in our galaxy, so we must make corrections to the GS," declared the head Reptilian.

"But now we have a big problem. How do we explain only eleven ambassadors returning to the Thorne Stargate to be sent home? There will be many questions and a thorough investigation," Striker stated.

"That is easy to rectify. All we have to do is send a replacement from my galaxy to the Stargate once we fix the GS," the Reptilian's condescending tone was noted by all.

"Won't my government discover that he is not the same Reptilian who came here with the other eleven?" asked Striker.

"Drax will select a replacement who looks very much like the one who died and he will have the identical computer ID chips and other documents," countered the Reptilian.

"Yes, I guess you guys all look alike," smirked Striker.

"Your obvious racist comment and attitude are neither appreciated nor helping to resolve this issue," the Reptilian was now visibly angry.

Striker and the head Reptilian spent several hours together working out the details of correcting the GS. Several attempts at sending small objects and animals through the Stargate failed. On the twenty-first attempt they succeeded and were ready for a human test subject. The head Reptilian alerted Drax and a replacement ambassador was sent from Drax's galaxy to Striker's Stargate.

The traditional rumble was felt through the cave, reaching an earthquake-like crescendo. Everyone observed the entire Stargate glowing. Suddenly, the glowing and rumbling subsided and with a final leap, a figure came through the circle like a dolphin soaring through a hoop. He landed on his stomach and slowly positioned himself to his hands and knees. Then he collapsed.

Four of the other Reptilians approached the traveler and helped him to his feet. They guided him to a couch and gave him a purple liquid drink, which quickly revived the traveler.

Now Striker was satisfied. The Stargate was operational and this would serve as his ticket to Drax's, galaxy upon the successful execution of the destruction of Earth's galaxy.

Meanwhile, back in Woodland Hills, Bob and Michele continue their discussion.

"Why can't he just return a few years before 3567 and obtain transportation from there?" Michele asked.

"That is precisely what we think he will do. Fortunately, we can trace him no matter which year he goes to," responded Bob.

Nova teleported the equipment Bob requested. One of the pieces of equipment Bob received was the Timeline Sequence Scanner (TSS), which he spent several minutes adjusting while Michele observed.

"Bob, what is that device? I have not seen it before."

"It's a Timeline Sequence Scanner, or TSS as I call it."

"What does it do?"

"The TSS allows me to view a past event that we didn't observe from the perspective of all events. This way we can see precisely what Striker did to create the three ripple points."

"You mean we can see exactly what he did even when you or both of us were at different locations?"

"Precisely. Now I need a few more minutes to adjust this so we can see what he did in 1945."

When Bob completed his adjustments to the TSS they both observed Striker sabotaging the fuses of both the "Little Boy" uranium bomb and the "Fat Man" plutonium bomb. These scenes viewed holographically totally amazed Michele. The wonders of the 36th-century technology always kept her attention and filled her with awe.

Now Bob and Michele teleported back to Los Alamos in 1945. Bob explained that they both would be seeing Bob's and Striker's parallel selves on this parallel universe. It was now July 16 and Michele watched as Bob placed some sort of computer chip-like strip, undetectable to the naked eye, on the fuses of both the "Little Boy" uranium bomb and the "Fat Man" plutonium bomb. Bob explained to Michele that this would alert them as to when Striker would sabotage the bombs.

"So what exactly is our plan, Bob?"

"We will let Striker sabotage the fuses and think everything is according to his plan. Then we will undo his sabotage and allow history on this parallel universe to proceed as we recorded it originally on our universe."

"Won't Striker know that we corrected the bomb's fuses?"

"No. Remember we can trace him, but he can't trace us. That also applies to his parallel self."

"What about your parallel self? Isn't this going to be a bit confusing?"

"No. I can communicate with my parallel self and alert parallel Bob as to what is going on and who I am."

Bob knew precisely when Striker would act. He prepared Michele for his actions and stressed the importance of parallel Striker being kept ignorant of their actions. Bob was concerned that parallel Striker would communicate with Striker, which could result in Striker returning to 1945 and the two other time eras to frustrate Bob and Michele's attempts to keep history correct on these parallel universes.

In addition to the obvious reasons, Bob was

concerned that any complications in his plan would make it more difficult for him to enact the patching procedure with the TSNU. Bob communicated with parallel Bob with the timeline synergizer and briefed the latter with instructions not to interfere. Bob and Michele's lives would also be in danger if Striker teleported to this parallel universe to assist parallel Striker.

Bob's plan was simple and relatively easy to enact. He and Michele simply waited for his computer chip-like strip to alert him as to Striker's actions. When that moment occurred Bob and Michele waited a few hours and teleported to the bomb's location and repaired the fuses. Parallel Bob did as he was instructed.

Parallel Striker was completely unaware of what took place. He returned to 2005 happy with what he now assumed was the successful sabotage of the Manhattan Project. Little did he know that Bob and Michele were in the fifth dimension of 1945 and placing exotic matter in a corridor of hyperspace.

Bob made some final adjustments to the TSNU and then activated it. A kind of light show resulted and after a few minutes Bob and Michele teleported to 1780.

"Do you think the TSNU successfully patched the ripple point Striker created in our universe?" Michele asked.

"I really don't know. I guess only time will tell," he mused.

"That plan seems to have worked quite well. Do you expect similar results in 1780 New York, Bob?"

"Our next step is far more complex. I'm going to need your help, so be prepared for a challenge."

Bob then sent a copy of his adjustments to the TSNU to Nova and waited for her reply. By the time Bob and Michele arrived in 1780 New York, Nova's response was communicated to Bob. She reported that history on that parallel universe remained unchanged and the relatively small ripple point that was created as a result of Striker's actions on our universe was repaired.

"Well, Michele, Nova has informed me that we were successful in 1945. That's one down and two to go."

"That's great! You don't seem that happy, why?"

"As I told you, Michele, 1945 was easy. We are now going to a more significant ripple point. If parallel Striker communicates with Striker and he teleports back to 1780, events will become far more difficult and complex."

As Bob and Michele arrived in Rockland County, New York, in 1780, they stayed in the fifth dimension while Bob used his TSS to observe what took place in their own universe as a result of Striker's actions. They watched a hologram presentation scanning the events Striker was directly involved with.

Bob and Michele observed the details that they could not see during their previous teleportation back to 1780. They noted Striker's presence in the fifth dimension observing the soldiers at Washington's headquarters at Tappan just prior to their attempt to arrest Major André.

"Why is the signal so poor, Bob?"

"The TSS doesn't work well with signals originating from the fifth dimension. We only knew that

Striker was listening to the soldiers at Tappan. Whatever action he took in the fifth dimension are unfortunately undetectable.

"The TSS was very clear in showing Striker's appearance from the fifth dimension and his murder of the three American soldiers as they were arresting Major André. They observed themselves coming onto the scene after the fact. Finally, Striker's following General Washington on the latter's trip to see Benedict Arnold was depicted clearly." Both Bob and Michele observed Striker's murder of George Washington with the phaser.

"So what is our plan, Bob?"

"First I will use the timeline synergizer to communicate with parallel Bob and Michele to alert them as to our presence and instruct them not to interfere."

"Why not have them come in on our side?"

"We already outnumber parallel Striker two to one. Four of us will just confuse the issue and be impossible to explain to the locals, should our actions be observed."

Bob then spent several minutes briefing parallel Bob as to the situation and Bob's plan. Next Bob communicated with one of the captains at Tappan and informed him in his dream state of Beverly Robinson's presence at the hotel.

"How did you do that, Bob? I mean guiding the captain at Tappan."

"Michele, all of our dreams are in reality trips to the fifth dimension. I simply placed myself in the captain's dream and advised him. This is what most people refer to as inspiration or intuition."

"Do you think parallel Striker is aware of our

presence in this parallel universe?"

"Not likely. The only way he could know of us is if Striker communicated with him and I don't see how that would be possible. It will be awhile before Striker finds out about our success in 1945. That is why we must act fast."

"Do you really believe Striker is that ignorant of our actions?"

"Yes, Michele. You see, he has a lot on his mind. There is Otto's arrest warrant, the FBI's investigation of Mannaco, the Mafia and threats from Drax."

Bob's communication with the captain at Tappan did result in Beverly Robinson's arrest. Their next move was to teleport to the site of Major André's arrest and prevent Striker from murdering the three American soldiers. From Bob's TSS of the arrest scene he knew precisely when Striker would attack.

Just as Striker arrived on the scene Bob placed the three American soldiers and Major André in suspended animation by way of the luminous red ball device. Michele fired her phaser at Striker and a cloud of dust was created as the phaser hit the dirt directly in front of Striker.

"You may have won this battle, Michele, but the war goes on. Give my best to Bob," Striker announced.

With that remark he returned to the fifth dimension. Bob approached Michele and immediately informed her of their next location. Just prior to Bob and Michele's returning to the fifth dimension, Bob removed the three American soldiers and Major André from suspended animation. The three soldiers arrested André and brought him to the Tappan headquarters.

"Now what, Bob?"

"We will go to Tappan and follow General Washington on his trip to see Benedict Arnold. Remember, Striker must return to the three-dimensional world to assassinate him. He cannot harm him from the fifth dimension."

Bob again had the advantage over parallel Striker in knowing precisely when he would kill Washington. It wasn't long before parallel Striker appeared and was confronted by Michele.

"You aren't going to kill anyone, buddy!" exclaimed Michele.

"Just watch me," declared Striker. He now fired his phaser at Michele. His shot missed and as he was distracted Bob fired his phaser that wounded parallel Striker in the leg. Just as parallel Striker disappeared to the fifth dimension he removed an odd-looking device from his pocket and spoke into it.

General Washington arrived several minutes later and Bob and Michele followed him to the fort, observing him from the fifth dimension. Washington knew nothing of what had taken place on the road to the fort. Benedict Arnold fled from the fort and history proceeded normally in this parallel universe.

Bob then placed some exotic matter in the corridor of hyperspace, adjusted the TSNU and fired his phaser at the exotic matter to patch the ripple point. He informed Nova immediately of his progress.

"Bob, you don't look happy. We just succeeded in thwarting parallel Striker twice."

"I don't doubt the patching will be successful. It's that device parallel Striker used that's bothering me."

"Yes, I noticed it too. It looked weird. What is it?"

"I just remembered that when I inventoried Taatos' lab prior to teleporting to 2005, one item on that list seemed out of place."

"What item was that, Bob?"

"It's that odd-looking device. That is the first timeline synergizer. Taatos developed it in 3050 to allow communication between parallel universe chrononauts. He was so far ahead of his time."

"So that means that parallel Striker has informed Striker as to our actions."

"Yes, Michele. Now Striker will teleport back to 1275 B.C. to prevent us from patching the ripple point. Up to now things have been relatively simple, but now we no longer have the advantage of surprise."

"But Bob, it's still four of us against two of him. Don't we still have the advantage?"

"Yes, we do. Striker doesn't have a TSS, so he will have to function from memory. In addition, he can't trace our teleportation and won't know where we will be or when."

"How do you know Striker doesn't have a TSS?"

"The TSS wasn't invented until the 33rd-century. It was not in Taatos' lab and there is no way an ambassador could obtain one. He probably doesn't know they exist."

Just then Bob received a message from Nova informing him that the second patching was successful and the black hole in the 36th-century was shrinking in size, but still very dangerous.

Bob and Michele teleported back to 1215 B.C. to observe the Battle of Jericho. They used the TSS to overview Striker's actions. They saw Striker killing one of the Hebrews and stealing his clothes. During this struggle Striker's phaser is rendered useless. Now Striker's morphed appearance was made clear.

The next scenes involved Bob and Michele arriving at Joshua's camp on the eastern bank of the Jordan River. Michele was seen guarding the Ark while Bob followed the two Jewish spies to Jericho. For six days the Hebrew soldiers surrounded the city of Jericho at dawn.

Both of these time travelers then observed Striker grabbing Michele from behind and knocking her unconscious with a block of wood. Striker then stole her phaser and returned to the fifth dimension following Bob's phaser shot at Striker's feet.

On the seventh day Bob was seen standing by the Ark while Michele was looking for Striker at Jericho. They observed the Levi priests lifting the Ark, praying to their God and lifting their trumpets. Suddenly, Striker appeared as a luminescent white being in front of the Ark and declared, "People of Israel you have disappointed me for the last time. I hereby abandon you now and forever." Striker then destroyed the Ark with Michele's phaser and returned to the fifth dimension.

"Have you devised a plan to deal with Striker, Bob?"

"You mean the two Strikers now. Our Striker will

be joining parallel Striker. It's now four against two. Yes, I have a plan."

Bob's plan began with preventing parallel Striker from grabbing Michele from behind, knocking her unconscious and stealing her phaser. Bob and Michele teleported to that location just prior to parallel Striker's appearance. A long and detailed contact with parallel Bob by Bob preceded this action. Parallel Bob and parallel Michele were briefed as to Bob's plan and what to do and what not to do. Basically, Bob's instructions consisted of having their parallel selves act as they planned and allow Bob and Michele to independently monitor the attack and act accordingly.

Bob and Michele teleported to the location where Striker attacked Michele. Unfortunately, they arrived just after parallel Striker knocked out parallel Michele and stole her phaser. Bob now stunned parallel Striker, while Michele attended to parallel Michele. Striker then appeared and fired his phaser at Bob's chest, mortally wounding him.

Striker then teleported to the fifth dimension with the stunned parallel Striker. Parallel Bob appeared on the scene and saved Bob's life through the use of his quantum laser device, applying the principles of quantum medicine. It took a few minutes for Bob to revive. Meanwhile in the fifth dimension parallel Striker was no longer stunned and the two Strikers continued to plot the destruction of the Ark.

Bob thanked parallel Bob for saving his life (it's weird to thank yourself!) and again instructed him and parallel Michele to continue with their previous plan.

Then Bob and Michele teleported to the seventh day of the Battle of Jericho and remained in the fifth dimension.

"Are you OK, Bob? You almost died earlier."

"I'm fine now, thanks to my parallel self's utilization of quantum medicine. Thanks for your concern."

"What's our plan now?"

"Now things get very complicated, as I warned earlier. Since parallel Striker and Striker are now both in the fifth dimension, I can trace them."

"Then what, Bob?"

"You see around you now in the corridors of hyperspace swirling lights and sudden flashes of color."

"Yes, Bob, I see them."

"If you will note the black voids you will see they function as entry and exit points to the fifth dimension. I can create a magnetic field with my TSNU and trap the Strikers."

"I don't understand, Bob. Please explain."

"You see, hyperspace physics teaches us that the only thing that can contain a fifth-dimensional object or being in hyperspace are magnetic fields and thought patterns. I will use these magnetic fields, along with thought patterns derived from my training in hypnosis and other spiritual methods, to confine the Strikers."

"Have you performed this technique before, Bob?"

"No, it's strictly theoretical. I'm confident it will work, as did my experimental adjustments to the TSNU to patch two of the ripple points."

"I can't argue with that success, Bob. What do you want me to do?"

"Just follow me with your phaser drawn and function as a distraction if things get tense."

Bob tracked the two Strikers to a certain corridor in hyperspace and he and Michele confronted the two Strikers. Michele fired her phaser at Striker while Bob quickly established the magnetic field. Parallel Striker escaped through one of the black voids and entered into another corridor in the fifth dimension.

Bob knew he and Michele had to go after parallel Striker. The magnetic field and thought pattern technique Bob initiated with Striker would only detain him for two hours. Bob knew that would be enough time to deal with parallel Striker. From this fifth-dimensional prison, Striker would be able to observe the Battle of Jericho.

Michele now rejoined Bob and they both teleported to the precise moment parallel Striker would make his appearance. Parallel Bob and parallel Michele continued with their role and Michele kept an eye out for any possible (though unlikely) interference from Striker.

They both observed parallel Striker's luminescent white image appearing and parallel Striker's declaration:

"People of Israel, you have disappointed me for the last time. I hereby abandon you now and forever."

With that last remark Bob fired his phaser at parallel Striker's right hand and observed parallel Striker's phaser drop to the ground. Parallel Striker's face was grimacing from the pain he was in from his leg wound and this made his voice sound weak.

Now Bob appeared as an even more luminescent white image dressed in his traditional white robe and stated: "Behold, I am the true God of the Jewish people. You are a false God and I will smite you in front of all the people."

With that last statement both Bob and Michele fired their phasers at parallel Striker, killing him and blasting his atoms into the air. Striker in the fifth dimension observed this scene, and cursed them both and quickly teleported back to 2005 when the magnetic field disappeared.

Bob and Michele observed the Hebrew soldiers and the others in awe of what they assumed to be the action of their God. Next, Bob and Michele returned to the fifth dimension where Bob initiated the patching procedure with exotic matter and the TSNU.

As Bob and Michele teleported back to 2005, all Michele could think about was the marvelous technology and experience she just shared with the time traveler who calls himself Bob Gullon. She never knew that history could actually be changed, not by altering events in our current universe, but in a parallel timeline.

It was totally inconceivable to her that altering the events of a parallel universe or timeline would interact with sister universes by way of parallel world gateways and these corridors in hyperspace were the precise location of ripple points.

The patching Bob did of these ripple points in the parallel world gateways through the use of the TSNU device, along with exotic matter, created a light show display that was just impossible to ignore.

Did Bob actually succeed in this patching the last ripple point Striker created? Only time would tell and they were quickly running out of time. Michele was impressed by Bob's ingenuity and resourcefulness in making adjustments to the TSNU. She didn't understand what he was doing, but somehow psychically felt that he had succeeded in this mission.

Michele learned a long time ago to trust her instincts, especially her psychic ones. When they arrived back in Woodland Hills Michele could sense a certain relief projected by Bob's presence and his energy. Bob spent two hours debriefing Michele.

As Striker returned from 1275 B.C. Israel to his Calabasas home, he felt frustrated. Even with the death of parallel Striker, a blow to his maniacal ego, Striker felt he had still succeeded in his plan. He was unaware of Bob's ripple point patching and in his own mind he had set into motion the destruction of the galaxy. Now he felt comfortable in reviewing several holographic messages Drax had sent him.

There were six messages ranging from requests of his progress to death threats. Striker did not concern himself with the first six. He laughed as he played them. It was the last message that added to his present state of mind.

"STRIKER YOU HAVE DONE BETTER THAN EVEN I EXPECTED. IGNORE MY PREVIOUS MESSAGES. WE ARE AWAITING YOUR ARRIVAL. ALL IS ARRANGED."

As Striker read Drax's body language during this transmission, he felt it was sincere. What Striker didn't realize was that Drax was a better actor than Striker could possibly imagine. If only Striker knew the mode of death Drax arranged for him upon his arrival. That is what Drax meant when he stated, "All is arranged."

The one problem that Striker faced before his departure was Otto Schmidt. Otto was cooped up in the Calabasas home for several days now and constantly complaining about his situation. Striker didn't care about the arrest warrant issued by the feds for Otto. That was his problem.

Striker's ego disliked the fact that Mannaco was in danger of being taken over by the government for his illegal activities. He knew none of this really mattered. Soon he would be back in the 36th-century briefly on Earth and then shortly across the galaxy.

"Boss, I'm worried. The feds are after me and I can't stay here twidddlin' my thumbs forever," Otto remarked.

"Don't worry, Otto. I will shortly see to it that nobody will bother you. My political contacts are now arranging for you to be relocated to a country which does not have extradition rights with the U.S. That means the feds can't arrest you," he lied.

"But what will I do?" Otto now seemed to be in a panic state of mind.

"I will transfer one hundred million dollars into a numbered Swiss account for you to use as you please. Think of yourself as an independently wealthy retired businessman. You can live quite comfortably on these funds, can you not?"

"Yeah, sure, but I won't be able to go anywhere."

"I will provide you with a list of dozens of countries you can visit without worry about extradition.

Your new passport with your new identity will stand any inspection." Striker was now tiring of this conversation. Nothing he said was true and all he cared about was making his own escape from 2005.

"Look, Otto, I'm tired from my recent trip. I'm going to bed. We will continue this discussion tomorrow."

What a difference a day makes. The patching technique initiated by Bob as a result of his and Michele's three trips back in time miraculously worked. The black hole in 3567 disappeared and to that time it never happened. Striker wasn't aware of any of this, but Drax was immediately informed of this situation. His next message to Striker was quite different.

"THE BLACK HOLE IS GONE AND SO IS MY PATIENCE WITH YOU STRIKER. YOU ARE A DEAD MAN."

As Striker received this message he racked his brain for a solution. He began to fiddle with the teleporter and removed the backing. As he stared at the extra computer chip it contained, he had an idea.

Fourteen

Following their arrival in Woodland Hills in 2005 both Bob and Michele felt drained. They went to their respective bedrooms for a well-earned rest.

Bob knew it would take several hours for the time patching to work, if it were to work at all. He would simply wait for Nova's communication. Michele went to her office the following morning and received a call from the LAPD. They investigated a shooting at a nightclub in Sherman Oaks and described the incident involving Otto.

Since there was a warrant out for Otto's arrest by the feds, Michele was alerted. The thug who got away was identified as Angelo Carlotti, a member of the DeNardo's New York gang.

Michele went to the scene with a rather unusual piece of equipment. Bob briefed her on the DNA sensor. This small pen-like device traces the DNA of an individual and can lead you to their present location.

Because Angelo's fingerprints were found in the club, the LAPD easily identified him. Michele took a small sample of the blood he left on the floor where he fell and placed it in the DNA sensor.

Shortly, a homing signal emerged form this device and Michele was on her way to arrest Angelo. She called her office for backup and within thirty minutes a motel room in North Hollywood was surrounded with FBI agents. Angelo came out with his hands up and Michele followed the other agents back to her office.

This was a break in the case against Mannaco. Michele knew that Angelo would be interrogated by some tough FBI agents and pressured to cut a deal. If Angelo turned state's evidence, this could lead to an indictment of Striker and Mannaco.

In the old days the Mafia lived by a code of silence. They would never squeal on anyone in their organization. Things have changed. Many captured Mafia criminals have turned in their colleagues for lighter sentences. Several have been placed in witness protection programs to assist in state and federal prosecution of crime families.

Michele went back to Woodland Hills feeling pretty good. She briefed Bob about the Angelo arrest and he seemed truly happy for her. Bob was somewhat preoccupied in finding out a way to locate and arrest Striker. Neither he nor the FBI had any idea where Striker's home was, or even if he still was in Los Angeles.

After a long hard day Michele liked to go jogging

and this day was no exception. She changed into her jogging outfit and headed out to Serania Park near the house to do some serious running. It would have been difficult for Michele to see the black helicopter directly above her. The silence of this advanced helicopter made it easy for Otto to descend and throw a gas bomb directly at Michele's feet. She was unconscious immediately.

Otto wore a gas mask, and when he placed Michele in the chopper quickly tied her up and placed tape over her mouth. He knew she would be out for an hour or so. Then Otto removed his mask and headed back to Striker's house.

When Michele awoke she was tied to a chair in Striker's library. She quickly scanned the large room and observed that only Otto and Striker were present.

"Are we alone, guys?"

"Yes, Michele. It's only us two and you. My security setup around this estate is all automatic. The security cameras alert robotic machine gunners who are built to shoot intruders on sight."

"How the hell did you find me, Otto?" Michele asked.

"My criminal contact informed me that you were seen recently several times jogging in Serania Park, so I just waited."

"You are both under arrest. I would like to read you your rights, but I am somewhat tied up at the moment."

Striker and Otto laughed and Striker pulled up a seat directly in front of Michele.

"You see, Peterman, I don't care much for you.

It's Bob I want."

"And just how do you think you're going to get him. He's a lot smarter and more resourceful than you, Striker."

"Oh yes, the patching he did to undo my three ripple points. That was brilliant and resourceful I must admit. It won't do him much good when I kill both of you."

"You might very well kill me, Striker, but you don't scare me. Just how are you going to get Bob?"

"The trap has already been set and you are the bait."

"Me?"

"Yes, you. I know Bob would have planted a tracer biochip on you, so it's just a matter of time before he shows up."

"Why not kill me right now?"

"That would simply not do. The biochip is only active as long as you are alive."

Michele realized instantly that she was in deep trouble. She didn't care so much for herself as for Bob. There must be a way to stop Striker, she thought to herself.

Bob became suspicious when Michele failed to return in an hour. She was never gone longer than that when she went jogging. He tried to locate her from the biochip he implanted, but was receiving quite a bit of static from his detector. She must be near a lot of machinery requiring a huge power source.

The signal did show that she was within a ten-mile radius, so Bob decided to drive around in the MR2 in order to zero in on her location. He brought the exotic matter Nova teleported him, his phaser, teleporter and quantum laser (concealed in his pants pocket) with him as he headed out of the driveway.

"Aren't you going to use the ANI on my brain to see what I know?" Michele asked.

"No, blondie, we know you know nothing. Honey, you are just a dumb bitch who is being used as bait," Otto grumbled.

"Now now, Otto, show the doomed federal agent respect on the last day of her life," Striker added.

Bob drove west following the signal and turned off at a Calabasas exit from the 101 Freeway. As he drove along a winding road snaking its way through lush rolling hills covered with trees, he approached a closed wrought iron gate. There were security cameras at several locations and some unidentified metallic objects hidden behind the gate.

Bob used one of his devices to render useless each of these pieces of equipment. The security monitors inside the house were blank and the robot machine gunners were now nothing more than statues.

It was not difficult to open the gate and drive up a winding two-lane private road to Striker's home. Bob was amazed to see such a large structure. Striker's home resembled a monastery with white stucco walls and red tile roofs. There was a black helicopter sitting on a pad off to the side of this massive building.

Now Bob decided to teleport into the house to try to surprise Striker. Ever since the security monitors went blank, Striker and Otto were alerted to Bob's presence.

Bob appeared just outside of the study and slowly moved toward it as he heard voices. Bob couldn't see Otto's hand come down and hit him on the back of the head with Otto's spare Walther PPK gun butt.

The next thing Bob became aware of was being brought to Striker's study at gunpoint by Otto.

"Oh, I am surprised. I did not think you would have the courage to break into my house," gloated Striker.

"I came here to rescue Michele and place you under arrest, Striker," responded Bob.

"Your jokes are not as funny as that of your cohort Michele Peterman. Bring her in, Otto," ordered Striker.

Otto brought in Michele while Striker pointed his phaser at Bob.

"You see, Bob, I want you and Michele to personally witness the beginning of the destruction of our galaxy. Both of you will have a bird's-eye view, too close for your own comfort."

"Instead of just killing us now, you want us to witness your master plan. But Striker, I patched all three of your ripple points. Your plan failed."

"Bob, as you know I have a brilliant criminal mind. And all brilliant criminal minds devise a backup plan. A plan B as it is called."

"And your plan B, what is it?"

"All in good time, my dear fellow. We will adjourn to my special underground laboratory. All will be fully explained shortly."

Otto removed Bob's jacket and carried it as he pointed his gun at Michele, while Striker aimed his phaser at Bob as they went to a large elevator at the end of the hall. Striker inserted his cardkey into the card reader and pressed the button labeled "A."

As all four exited the elevator they found themselves in a concrete corridor leading to a large lab. They passed through a set of glass doors leading to a long hallway, then through a second set of glass doors opening into a lab with doors opening off either side. Each of the doors was designed to slide open on a motorized track.

Striker had Otto keep an eye on Bob and Michele as he pointed to a computer room packed with high-tech equipment. Adjacent to this room was a large machine with an open tube large enough for several people to pass through.

"Let me guess, Striker, this is the Wormhole Linear Accelerator you stole from Taatos' lab," Bob surmised.

"You are correct. This museum piece was the most powerful superconductor conceived in its day. It handled over ten trillion electron volts of energy. The very fabric of space-time can be manipulated with this ancient device," gloated Striker.

"I don't see how an inoperable WLA is going to help you, Striker. Right now in 3567 Drax is really pissed at you," commented Bob.

"Science has always posed risks to humanity. We count on our wisdom and maturity to keep up with our pursuit of knowledge. We both know enough about hyperspace physics to be aware that ripple points can create large tears in the fabric of space-time and cause the destruction of our galaxy."

"But I patched the three ripple points you created, jerk, so why are you so happy?"

"Yes, that is true," Striker's face was set in a vengeful mask, showing no trace of mercy.

"Striker, in addition to all of your crimes you committed a crime of omission. No workable WLA means no plan B," Bob exclaimed.

As Bob looked at he WLA he observed heavy black power cables snaking around the entire unit. The dull gray color of the machine hummed softly as it became bathed in a violent light. A mist of white vapor appeared to surround the unit. The air in the lab was cold with a slight musty odor. Bob could almost see his breath as he planned his next move. The electrical transformer to the right of the WLA appeared to be a power source to these black cables.

"I can see schematics of the WLA on the computer screen and a whole bunch of smoke and mirrors, but it does you no good without the special computer chips needed to work this contraption," added Bob.

All the while Michele kept a vigilant eye on Otto and looked for an opportunity to somehow overpower him. Suddenly, a loud screeching sound appeared to come from the computer console directly behind the WLA. Both Striker and Otto turned to check it out when Michele tackled Otto and Bob knocked Striker's phaser from his hand.

Striker ran out one of the side doors of the lab into a labyrinth of corridors with Bob running behind him. Bob made a turn into a different corridor and realized he had lost Striker and didn't know how to get back to the lab. He cursed the fact that he neglected to retrieve his phaser.

Back in the lab Michele and Otto were fighting it out. Michele was smaller than Otto, but faster and smarter. Neither of them had weapons, so their struggle consisted of hand-to-hand combat.

Michele used her karate kicks and chops to weaken Otto, but he wouldn't give up. Now Otto began to corner Michele by the transformer next to the WLA. He moved in on her and she was trapped.

Bob finally figured out which corridor led to the lab and ran as fast as he could to save Michele and teleport the WLA back to the 36th-century. As he entered the lab, Otto was right on top of Michele. He pushed her into the transformer and quickly pulled down a master switch.

Bob screamed "No" at the top of his lungs as he watched Michele fall dead to the ground, electrocuted. Otto saw Bob and quickly exited through another glass door leading from the lab.

Bob quickly checked Michele's body and saw that she was dead. He noted the time on the lab clock and raced after Otto. Otto reached the elevator first and ran through the house on his way out to the helicopter pad.

Bob finally exited the house himself in time to see Otto take off in the black helicopter. It took merely a few seconds for Bob to aim and fire Striker's phaser at the helicopter as soon as it reached the height of about one hundred feet. The chopper exploded and Otto fell to the Earth, dead long before his body hit the ground.

Bob glanced at his watch and headed back to the

lab. He had less than an hour to use his quantum laser to bring Michele back to life. "Thank God for quantum medicine and 36th-century technology," he thought.

Bob ran as fast as he could to get back to the lab. The elevator door was open when he approached it. He pressed the A button, feeling adrenaline surging through his body. Bob cursed as he realized he'd neglected to bring his teleporter with him. As he reached the lab he froze, as his body became numb and he lost consciousness. Striker came out from behind a computer console holding Bob's phaser set on stun.

The next thing Bob was aware of when he regained consciousness was being handcuffed to a chair within twenty feet of the WLA and Striker sitting on a chair opposite him.

"Welcome back to the waking world, Bob. Isn't it ironic that I used Michele's handcuffs to immobilize you in that chair? Who would have thought an FBI special agent would carry handcuffs in her running jacket?"

Bob scanned the lab quickly and observed his jacket with his teleporter lying next to the WLA. He saw Michele's body in front of the transformer and tries to devise a plan to salvage this seemingly hopeless situation.

Striker then moved to the main console and checked video readings in front of him. He then flipped a switch and a dense array of lasers appeared in the center of the WLA. Bob could then see a succession of hyperspace physics calculations move across the screen at a rapid rate.

As Bob tried to hide his frustration with words, he

felt the possibility of any advantage slipping away.
"Your machine can't work, Striker."

"It's nice to be consistent in a city of inconsistencies, Bob. You will shortly learn the fallacies of your remarks."

"The way I hear it you and Mannaco are through. You are a wanted man and the FBI is all over your company," Bob stated emphatically.

Striker's face darkened with anger and his reply held a brittle edge. "You and Peterman have been a thorn in my side for the last time. She is dead and you will shortly join her. As for my plans, I will teleport back to 3567 and quickly relocate to Drax's galaxy for my reward."

"Striker, you sound almost nervous. Do you really think that lizard is going to be true to his word? By the way, how in God's name did you repair the WLA?"

"You see, my dear chrononaut, I used quantum technology to repair the WLA. The extra computer chip that comes with every teleporter applies the concept of using the quantum attributes of atoms."

"But Striker, the teleporter chip is based on 35th-century technology, while the WLA was developed using 31st-century hyperspace physics," Bob added.

"The quantum characteristics that the teleporter chip utilizes is based on utilizing all thirty-two quantum states of an electron. I only required twelve of those states for the WLA. So you can thank yourself and the use of your teleporter chip for my ability to repair and activate the WLA you see before you," gloated Striker.

"Striker, why am I still alive? Why didn't you just

kill me with your phaser, rather than merely stun me?"

"I want you to personally view the beginning of the destruction of our galaxy."

"You are insane, you know that," Bob responded.

"Sure I'm insane. I will be hysterically laughing all the way to a distant galaxy where I will be king!"

"Striker, how do you expect to travel to Drax's galaxy with our government after you big time?"

"My dear fellow, I will use a Stargate."

"There is only one Stargate on our planet, Striker. The Thorne Stargate, named after the 21st-century Cal Tech astrophysicist Kip Thorne is the most secure installation on the planet. You will never get by its security."

"Bob, you underestimate me. I am well aware of the Thorne Stargate and have no plans to use it."

"Then how will you leave our galaxy?"

"Remember the representatives from Drax's galaxy that paid us a visit through the Thorne Stargate several years ago?"

"Yes, Striker. What about it?"

"Well, those twelve men were scientists and with my assistance constructed a second Stargate unknown to the government. I will use that one, dear boy."

"You're bluffing, Striker."

"Not on our life, and I mean that literally. Isn't it ironic that a Stargate generates an artificial wormhole that will transport me to Drax's galaxy and I will use that WLA to destroy our galaxy?"

"So where is this Stargate, Striker?"

"All in due time. Right now I am more interested

in the WLA," Striker commented.

"So you have the WLA turned on. How long will it take to actually be activated and to begin the black hole generation process to be seen in the 36th-century?"

"Patience, dear boy. I call you a boy, but you are sixty-five years older than me. How ironic. To answer your question, it will take another fifteen minutes to become activated."

Bob's eyes quickly scanned the lab and he noted the precise location of the jacket he wore which contained enough exotic matter to prevent Striker's plan from succeeding. He decided to play along with Striker's megalomania until he could free himself.

"You know, Striker, your scientific genius and resourcefulness is to be applauded the way you repaired the WLA. There is no question in my mind that quantum theory is an accurate mathematical model for our universe. It's been confirmed repeatedly. There's just one thing this quantum theory can't explain which is critical to your plan."

"And just what is that, Bob?" Striker asked.

"Quantum mechanics fails to explain how a sick asshole like you ever became an ambassador."

With that remark Striker's face turned red and he shook his fist at Bob. By this time Bob had manipulated the quantum laser from his pants pocket into his right hand and raised the laser to cut through his handcuffs. As Striker approached Bob to punch him, Bob reached up and hit Striker across the latter's left jaw with enough force to send Striker stumbling across the room.

Bob jumped up and focused on the large clock in

the lab. It showed that Michele had been dead for forty minutes and Bob had only twenty minutes left to revive her with his quantum laser. In addition, the WLA was now activated and Bob had to somehow line it with the exotic matter in his jacket within the next fifteen minutes, or Striker's plan would succeed.

Striker approaches Bob now armed with his phaser. He tried to wield the weapon at Bob, but Bob was too quick for him. Before Striker can activate the phaser Bob overpowered him physically and sent the phaser flying across the room.

Striker became livid with anger. His face turned red and he stared at Bob.

"I want you to know that I killed a woman whom you loved. That woman was Tiana Closeau. Ring a bell?" Striker asked.

"So it was you who killed my fiancée! What in heaven's name could have motivated you to perform such an evil act?" Bob was now visibly angry.

"You see, dear boy, it was I who arranged for your meeting with Tiana that evening three years ago at the WFHA lecture. I blackmailed her. Tiana lied on her application to the embassy about her family background. She tried to hide the fact that she had an alcoholic, child-molesting father. The Embassy frowns upon such potential blackmail situations in our delicate negotiations. So when I discovered this fact I blackmailed her into establishing a relationship with you. I knew that would appeal to your knight-like sensibilities and that you would not report the fact to the embassy.

But what could you possibly gain by that?" Bob asked.

"My plan was to have you fall in love with her, which you did and then have her dump you."

"But why?" Bob was still confused.

"Do you remember that assignment you completed about four years ago when you arrested a spy from Drax's galaxy who tried to infiltrate the TTSA?"

"Yes, I do. She was a human living on one of the planets in Drax's galaxy and her mission was to sabotage the TTSA. So what?" Bob exclaimed.

"That spy and I had a secret affair. I loved her and your actions resulted in her execution. Now I wanted you to see bow it felt to lose someone you loved and who loved you."

"You truly are a sick man, Striker. Why kill Tiana?"

"She wouldn't dump you as ordered. The bitch fell for you and wanted to go through with the marriage."

"It will give me even more pleasure to rid our galaxy of you and your twisted mind," Bob declared.

Striker leaped at Bob and took a swing at him. Bob slammed the palm of his hand up against Striker's nose, sending the cartilage into Striker's brain. Striker dropped to the floor, blood pouring from his nose.

Bob looked at the clock. He only had ten minutes to stop the WLA from destroying the galaxy and fifteen minutes to save Michele. Bob raced to the phaser and picked it up as Striker got up from the floor and headed for the door leading out of the lab. Bob barely missed him with the phaser and Striker now moved right in front of the WLA. Bob ran up to him as Striker lunged for Bob again. Bob quickly dodged Striker and kicked Striker with such force that Striker was sent into the WLA.

Bob could now focus on the humming of the WLA as it grew louder. The base of the machine began to vibrate and squeal and the sounds were as loud as a scream. He noted a dense array of purple and blue lasers being fired into the center of the WLA. Striker's body appeared to glow and become elongated. Finally, there appeared a blinding flash of light, a loud scream from Striker and then silence. The flashes of light diminished in intensity, until there was nothing but darkness inside the WLA. Bob realized now that people had their own dying time.

Bob quickly took the pocket of exotic matter from his jacket and threw it into the entrance of the WLA. Then he aimed his phaser at the center of the packet and the packet exploded, lining the walls of the WLA. Just two minutes were left on the lab clock. He didn't know whether his plan worked and wouldn't find out until he contacted Nova later.

Now he had to act fast. Bob raced over to Michele's body and skillfully ran his quantum laser over it. The lab clock showed that he completed this task with fewer than thirty seconds before the hour expired from the time of Michele's death.

Bob could now feel Michele's entire body begin to tremble involuntarily. Finally, her eyes opened and she looked up at Bob. He was holding her in his arms and praying to himself that she would revive.

"You're going to be fine, my darling. Just rest for now. It will be a few minutes before you can walk," Bob said lovingly.

"What about Otto?" she asked.

"He's dead."

"And Striker?" she queried.

"Let's put it this way. Think of a taffy pull and the most burnt French fry you have ever seen. Striker is stretched, radiated and his atoms are shattered throughout the fifth dimension. Whatever is left of his body is vaporized."

Bob used his teleporter to return the WLA to Taatos' lab and waited for Michele to be able to walk before he guided her out to the MR2. He would update Nova on events and Striker's Stargate when he returned to Woodland Hills."

Sometime later in Drax's office a report was presented to him summarizing Striker's failure and the role Bob and Michele played in destroying Striker's plan.

"You've won this battle, chrononauts, but the war goes on. We will again engage in battle," Drax declared as his reptilian hands pounded on top of his desk. Next, Drax smiled a wicked smile because he knew that this was only a minor battle lost in a war he's destined to win.

Epilogue

Michele's interrogation of Angelo led to surprisingly good rewards. Not only did Angelo turn state's evidence and supply evidence to the FBI regarding Striker's money-laundering, but he gave the feds many leads to other witnesses and incriminating evidence involving the four crime families formerly headed by Fabrizio Romano, Vincenzo Bellani, Pasquale DeNardo and Lorenzo Giamona.

Mannaco was restructured. The FBI's investigation revealed that Mannaco's CFO and other officers had no involvement with the money-laundering, or murders perpetrated by Striker. Only Striker and Otto were involved and both of them were dead.

Assistant Director Drake Collins's attitude toward Michele changed drastically. He had seriously considered firing her and now he put in a commendation for his "star" special agent. Michele's attitude also underwent a noticeable metamorphosis. She no longer felt like a loser and she now earned a rest and the company of a man she was deeply attracted to, namely Bob.

Bob went with Michele to pick up Sheba and brought them back to Woodland Hills for a special dinner. This was to be a celebration of their success on the Striker mission.

Saving the galaxy does deserve a special meal. Bob refrained from ordering burgers and fries from In-N-Out Burger and instead ordered a gourmet dinner for two to be delivered to the Woodland Hills house.

Both Bob and Michele felt somewhat giddy. They had done nothing to deal with the growing sexual tension between them. Even before they sipped the champagne Bob ordered, a feeling of joy and lack of inhibitions enveloped both of them. Even Sheba could sense their joy as she purred repeatedly following her rubbing against Bob's legs under the dining room table.

Suddenly, Bob was alerted to a hologram message from Nova. He brought the receiver and transmitter into the dining room and awaited Nova's message.

"Well, hotshot, I see you are drinking champagne with Michele. You both have a lot to celebrate."

"What's been happening in 3567, Nova?"

"Everything is back to normal. It's as if nothing happened regarding the black hole."

"Fortunately, I kept a record of our communications, so you can prove what actually happened and what might have happened to the government," Bob responded.

"I still can't believe you succeeded in this large a patching with the Time Sequence Nullification Unit. Nobody has ever repaired so large a ripple point before."

"Nova, I will send you the specs on my adjustments to the unit. Anything else before Michele and I continue with our meal?"

"Yes, there are four things. First, I have cleared with the FBI Michele's extended leave so she can assist you with further assignments. Second, you are to remain in 2005 in your present location to handle these additional missions. The third is we are seeking the location of Striker's Stargate."

"And the fourth?" asked Bob.

"Oh, I almost forgot. Our research has revealed that Michele is your great, great, great, great....grandmother."

"What!" Bob exclaimed.

"You heard me, hotshot. We've known this for quite awhile. Why do you think we allowed her to teleport back in time with you?"

"But, it can't be!"

Both Bob and Michele appeared to turn white. The previous look of frivolity was now replaced by one of embarrassment.

"Yes it can and is, Bob. By the way, enjoy your meal. I'll be in touch."